The Celtic Tiger

from the outside looking in

Mary Valarasan-Toomey

This book was typeset by
Gough Typesetting Services for
BLACKHALL PUBLISHING
26 Eustace Street
Dublin 2
Ireland
e-mail: blackhall@tinet.ie

© M Toomey, 1998

ISBN: 1 901657 21 3

"You've got to be carefully taught"
Words and music by
Richard Rodgers and Oscar Hammerstein II
©1949, Williamson Music International, USA
Reproduced by permission of
EMI Music Publishing Ltd,
London, WC2H 0EA

A catalogue record for this book
is available from the British Library.
All rights reserved. No part of this publication may be reproduced, stored in a retrieval system or transmitted in any form or by any means, electronic, mechanical, photocopying, recording or otherwise, without the prior, written permission of the publisher.

This book is sold subject to the condition that it shall not, by way of trade or otherwise, be lent, resold, hired out, or otherwise circulated without the publisher's prior consent in any form of binding or cover other than that in which it is published and without a similar condition including this condition being imposed on the subsequent purchaser.

Printed in Ireland by
Betaprint

Foreword

Mary Valarasan-Toomey has been my very dear friend and wonderful neighbour for many years. She brings to her writing a clear and analytical mind, deep compassion and her usual great sense of humour.

Proud of her adopted nation and its heritage, she has never forgotten the land of her birth. This attitude gave her the ability to write this book with great freedom of expression and without any inhibition. It is an attempt to say "Thank you" to the Irish people for welcoming her as an immigrant 31 years ago. However, in the ensuing 31 years, she has observed a change in attitude to many of our values. This book looks at those changes in areas such as the family, education, the Church and, in particular, in relation to our attitude towards refugees and asylum-seekers.

She writes with great passion and a deep abhorrence of anything hypocritical. She is frightened by the growing intolerance towards foreigners: those who like herself, have been living here for many years and those who have recently come to our shores. They come from various cultures – cultures into which they have been born; in which they have been nurtured and which have become part of them. They know and understand no other. How can they? How can they be expected to understand the new and alien culture in which they now find themselves?

Christianity teaches that each human being is unique and has something special to offer. We need to reach out to those who have arrived on our soil seeking refuge with love and compassion and educate them in the ways of this new culture, so that they may understand and absorb it.

So, sharing is the main thrust of this book, sharing of knowledge, material things, money and culture. Sharing has always been a high priority for Mary Valarasan-Toomey and in this book she shares her joys, hopes and fears with us. We should ignore them at our peril.

Canon W S Gibbons
August 1998

Contents

Acknowledgements

In the course of writing this book I interviewed many people both to allow me to reflect on my own impressions and to gain different perspectives on the changes that have taken place over the past 30 years. I am particularly grateful to the following people who have given generously of their time: Peter Barry, Helen Dillon, Joan Burton, Dr Sultan Jinna, Rosemary and Derek Mitchell, The Very Rev Victor Griffin, Ann McLoughlin, Richard Wood, Declan Martin, The Venerable Robin E Bantry White, Fr Declan Mansfield and to the many refugees who for obvious reasons prefer not to be named. I am also grateful to Catherine MacHale who was instrumental in arranging some of the interviews.

I talked to a number of young people and students among whom I must thank David Waters, Paul Cummins and Mick Keane for giving me a comprehensive insight into the attitudes of today's 17-20-year-olds.

Although this book presents my personal views, I have tried to be historically accurate which necessitated a considerable amount of research. I was very fortunate in having the assistance of Paddy Ó Callanáin who gave unstintingly of his time searching newspaper and State archives verifying dates of significant events.

Gerry Glennan was helpful in compiling a summary of attitudes towards refugees and asylum-seekers as expressed on contemporary radio programmes. Claire Gloster and Aoife Toomey combed the newspapers for useful cuttings. Such research as I undertook personally, was greatly facilitated by the cheerful staff of the Gilbert Library, Dublin. To all of them my heartfelt thanks.

Many thanks also to Andy Pollak who generously allowed me to quote extensively from his paper on refugees – an address to Cleraun Media Conference held on 21 February 1998.

In addition, I wish to record my gratitude to Tony Mason and Claire Rourke of Blackhall Publishing, the first for encouraging me to write this book in the first place; the latter for her patience and thoroughness during the editing of the manuscript.

And finally I am deeply grateful to those whose contribution cannot be measured quantitatively but without whose support this book would never have seen the light of day. Thank you Joan Reilly, Rita Eustace, Dorothy Mills, Lillian Harris, Pat Kennedy, Mieke Scholte and Breda Roseingrave for your support and encouragement. Last but not least to my husband and friend Barry and my daughter Aoife, thank you for your forbearance.

Dedication

This book is dedicated to the memory of the late Rev Father John Gildea C.S.Sp who welcomed me into the Catholic Church and who, over three long decades, listened patiently to my abiding preoccupations: my quest for knowledge and education; my passion for peace in the land of my birth and my deep desire to return to my roots; peace in Northern Ireland; concern for people in the developing world, poverty and starvation; abhorrence of every kind of racism; hatred of charlatanism and materialism. He urged me not to lose any of my eastern traditions and values but to marry them with the best of the Irish ones and serve those in need to the best of my ability. I am deeply honoured to call this good man a friend and mentor.

I also dedicate this book to the refugees and asylum-seekers in Ireland with whom I identify, and whose pain, fear and anxiety I share.

Part of the proceeds from the sale of this book will be donated to Spiritan Asylum Services Ireland (SASI) specifically for *Educational Programmes for Refugees and Asylum-Seekers in Ireland.*

COLAISTE DHULAIGH
LIBRARY
COOLOCK

First Words

I always wanted to write a book about Ireland – to say "Thank you" to the people of Ireland. I wanted to write it with joy and always hoped to do it some day. That day arrived rather unexpectedly on 10 December 1997 after I delivered an emotional paper at a conference on "Ireland of the Welcomes – Refugees and Racism". Thirty years previously I would not have believed that there would be racism in Ireland or that I would stand on a podium in the heart of Dublin making a heartfelt appeal to the people of Ireland not to humiliate refugees and asylum-seekers.

The 'welcomes' – were they there at all? Engulfed by sadness and disappointment that this land of welcome is fast disappearing, I have put together my thoughts, feelings and opinions on topics, which were, and are, close to my heart. Thirty years of living and growing in a land I love so much gave me the freedom to reminisce, examine and question the past and the present. The future belongs to the young, and my daughter Aoife – an Irish woman and a Dubliner – looks into the millennium with her contribution to this book. It is my fervent hope that one day in the future she will pick up where I left and write about the next 30 years. May she, and many other young Irish people like her, never be made to feel unwelcome in their own native land that they proudly call Ireland.

The Irish people should rightly and deservedly take great pride and pleasure in all that they have contributed to my life as an immigrant. Thank you.

Map of Ceylon

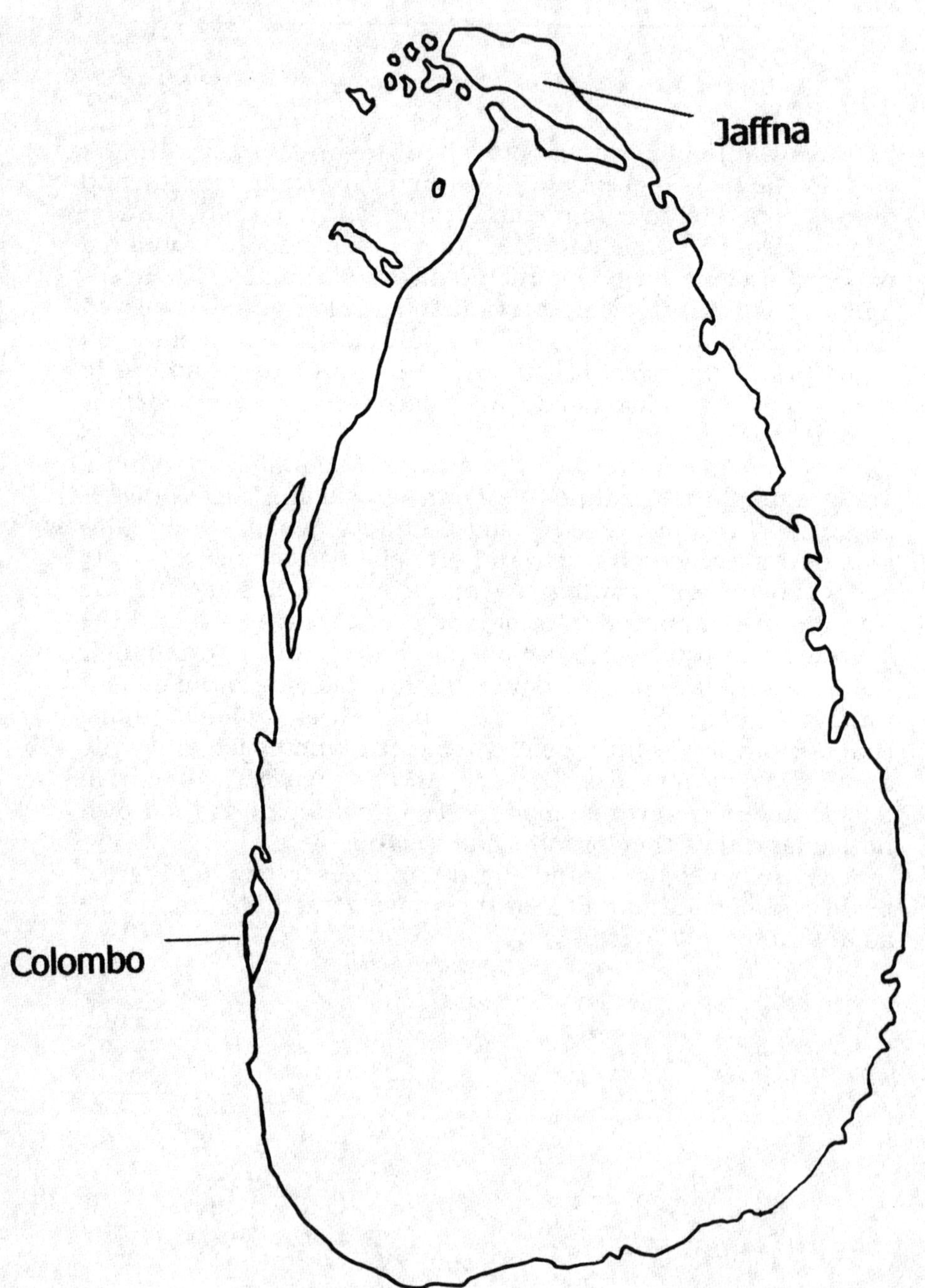

Publisher's Note

Throughout this book, the author refers to her homeland as Ceylon, even though it changed its name to Sri Lanka in 1972, with the adoption of a new constitution.

The island of Ceylon boasts a continuous human civilisation over two millennia and has been a centre of Buddhist culture from the 3rd century BC. As the ancient kingdom of Sinhala it was ruled by Sinhalese and Tamil kings and by a succession of invaders from southern India between the 3rd and the 12th centuries AD. In 1517 the Portuguese built a fort at Colombo (now the capital city) and by the end of the 16th century they controlled large sections of the island. In 1685 the Dutch gained control of most of the island, a position they maintained until 1798 when the island became a British Crown Colony. In 1948 Ceylon became an independent member of the British Commonwealth.

In 1955 a new Sinhala nationalism was unleashed and in 1960, the government of the Sri Lanka Freedom Party passed a Bill making the language of the majority Sinhalese community the only official language, thereby disqualifying most of the minority Tamil community, into which the author was born, from official appointments, including educaitonal and teaching positions. Although some concessions were subsequently made, the author, and many of her contemporaries emigrated to seek opportunities elsewhere. Relations between the Tamils and Sinhalese have been strained since 1960 and, in 1983, a civil war began between the Sinhalese-dominated government and the rebel Liberation Tigers of Tamil Eelam (LTTE). The LTTE is a group that seeks to create a separate nation for the Tamil minority in the northern and eastern provinces of Sri Lanka. Since fighting between the two groups began In 1983, about 40,000 people – from both communities – have been killed.

As a result of the civil war a large number of the minority Tamil population, including the rest of the author's family, have emigrated to Canada, Australia, the UK, Germany and Denmark. The author has no blood relatives living in Sri Lanka today.

All that is necessary for evil to triumph is that good men shall do nothing.

Edmund Burke

Chapter 1

Initial Impressions: the early years

July 1967: destination – Trinity College, Dublin. As the plane from Heathrow approached Dublin airport, I was very happy to see acres of green lush grass – no wonder Ireland is known as the 'Emerald Isle' I thought. The airport building appeared to be a modest one, nothing extraordinary, perhaps slightly larger than the airport in Colombo, capital of Ceylon (now known as Sri Lanka). From one island to another – little did I realise then that Ireland would still be my home 30 years on!

My mother, a school teacher and passionately fond of geography, had taught me about Ireland when I was at primary school, and the Irish nuns in my high school, Holy Family Convent, Jaffna (the town where I was born), never failed to sing the praises of their land and their school children: "Irish girls behaved very well, they would never run on the school corridors, they always walked like ladies, their manners were excellent . . ." These were Reverend Mother Principal's opening words at the school assembly at least once a month. I can still hear them, though I know now those words were not altogether true. For heaven sake school children are the same all over the world, aren't they? The Irish children I taught at the Sandymount High School, a very progressive co-educational school in the late-1960s and Loreto Convent in St Stephen's Green, were no different from the children in my old school in Jaffna.

What I could not understand was that the secondary school children in Ireland were not taught biology as a science subject, and there was also a dearth of science and biology teachers in the country. Strange indeed, but in a matter of a few months as I became involved in a number of second-level school teachers' courses on biology run by the Department of Education in association with the Zoology Department of Trinity College, I understood that human reproduction and matters pertaining to sex were not considered to be suitable topics of study for a long number of years. It was not until the 1970s that biology was introduced as a subject in the Leaving Certificate curriculum. Yet botany was a Leaving Certificate subject. I suppose it was all right to learn about plants and plant life, but not about bees, butterflies and sex.

Despite the fact that I was far away from everything that was familiar to me – my home, my family, long hours of warm sunshine throughout the year, tropical blue skies and splendid flora and fauna – I felt at home in the heart of Dublin and did not feel painfully homesick. I got to know Irish people very quickly. They were very friendly, always ready to greet me, have a pleasant conversation about my native country, my people and my language – always anxious to welcome the stranger and apologise for the Irish weather. How often had I heard the lament "all this rain and dampness; not enough sun . . . still, I hope you like living here . . . ".

I remember my first conversation with the postmistress in Clonskea post office. She was very pleased to talk to me, and at the same time was surprised that I could speak so clearly and precisely in English. I wondered why she should be pleased or surprised, after all English is more or less a universal language. However, I could see the lady was very happy to assume and articulate that the dedicated Irish nuns – the missionaries – had done a good job on me.

"God bless the good work our nuns and priests are doing here in Ireland and all over the world. What would we do without them?" she said with great pride.

Indeed I remember the nuns collecting money for the starving children in the developing world well before the television brought the sad and, at times harrowing images, of these suffering children into Irish homes. Such was the innocent, simple, caring and proud approach of the Irish to people in need, not only in their cities and counties, but also for those in other countries.

The Irish people always found time for everyone, be they neighbours, friends or acquaintances. I was struck by the ease and the speed with which they were able to befriend people like me, a stranger, a foreigner, and extend an invitation to tea or supper without hesitation. They took a great deal of trouble to make me feel very welcome in their homes and country. How can I ever forget my first Christmas in Ireland? That kind Moore Street lady from whom I bought my vegetables every Saturday insisted that I have afternoon tea with her in her modest dwelling, and I did. The important thing was that I was not afraid, I did not feel inhibited to accept the invitation, and was most impressed and touched by her thoughtfulness, generosity and kindness. She even had a little Christmas present for me. I kept in touch with her for a very long time.

Thanks to the generosity and kindness of another friend – an Irish nun I had met abroad – I had temporary accommodation in the homes of her family and friends for a few weeks after I arrived in Dublin. Two elderly sisters living in Marlborough Road, Donnybrook, introduced me to porridge, and I was fascinated by the special pot they used to make the porridge each morning. "Porridge is very good for you especially on cold frosty mornings," was the advice given to me by these kind ladies. Not being used to low temperatures, I suffered often from colds during my early days in Dublin. On one occasion when I was ill with a very severe cold, a friend with whom I was staying gave me a drink and advised me to stay in bed. I did not wake up for nearly two days – I did not realise it at the time, but this was my first encounter with poitín, often drunk as a cure for colds and flu – my cold was cured! Only later did I realise that poitín is an alcoholic drink, not legally available in Ireland.

Flat hunting was an enjoyable experience too. There was no major hunting really, though I was most anxious to live close to my friend's family. Donnybrook was also very convenient for travelling, the shops and the other essentials of life. My flat was nothing elaborate, but more than adequate for my needs. I found it very quickly, a bedsit, in 72 Morehampton Road. It was brand new, beautifully clean with a new, wall-to-wall carpet. The rent was £5 per week and the landlord could not do enough to make this place as comfortable as possible for me. My nationality, my creed, my colour, made no difference. He kept saying, "If only I could find more tenants like you – so polite, so well spoken, so warm and so friendly. If there are more students from your country studying in Dublin they will be welcome." An alcove with two front doors was my kitchenette! One Sunday I had invited a friend of mine from college to lunch, but forgot that I did not have a saucepan in which to cook my carrots. I had a frying pan and an aluminium teapot, so the carrots were cooked in the teapot – what fun we had, and the lunch was served elegantly.

After about three months, I found the bedsit too small and restrictive, even though it was within reach of every possible amenity. I therefore went in search of a more spacious and comfortable flat to share with two friends. My helpful landlord was disappointed but understood my predicament and wished me well. We managed to get a garden flat at 12 Northumberland Road. I could walk to college and my share of the rent was £7 a month. There was no central heating. The convector heater mounted on the wall of the small living room provided all the heat I needed to keep my tropical body warm, I had to ensure there were plenty of 2/– (approx. 10p) pieces to feed the electric meter.

The one thing I just could not get used to in Dublin was the bath. Having been accustomed to cold showers all my young life, I found sitting in the dirty bath water and getting out without showering myself down somewhat disconcerting. I also understood that not many Irish people had a bath every day. In the tropics, the heat and the humidity demanded a shower at least twice a day. Therefore, I was very pleased that the landlord of my new flat had installed a shower unit, he even asked me to go and choose the shower curtain in McKenzies of Pearse Street.

Young Irish readers of this account about my joys of having a shower unit in my flat may find it somewhat odd. The Ireland into which I arrived did not boast many homes with shower units or central heating. I was also very grateful to the landlord for a generous supply of Greenhills, white, cotton sheets, pillowcases and Foxford blankets. Beautifully starched, crisp, white, cotton bedsheets may be a thing of the past but what joy it was to slip between them. An abundant supply of them would be my luxury item on a desert island! Continental quilts had not arrived in the big stores then, though I did have an electric blanket – this was a sheer necessity because I loathed getting into a cold bed. I also found the coldness of the bathroom difficult to come to terms with – and wondered how people put up with the cold winters year after year.

The flat was not equipped with a washing machine – a luxury in those days – I had to do my washing and ironing each weekend. I was used to a family washerman (dhoby) my parents employed in Ceylon. Washing clothes by hand in a small sink was a very new experience for me, and one that I found difficult. Saturday mornings were spent at the Baggot Street launderette. I enjoyed my walks each Saturday from Northumberland Road via Haddington Road to Upper Baggot Street exchanging greetings with passers by and occasionally chatting with some. Time – there was no shortage of it – even if the weather was very cold, but the grey skies, rain and wind, bothered me for a long time.

Having a garden flat meant there was a back garden. Gardening was always a passionate hobby of mine, and therefore, I was able to garden whenever I had some free time especially during spring and summer. During my early years in Dublin, every front garden I looked at had a lawn, a tree or a shrub and perhaps a bed of roses or some summer flowers. Although enchanting, they were nothing sensational and I often missed the splendour and variety of the tropical flora of my own serendipitous island of Ceylon. Herbert Park and St Stephen's

Green became my garden – they were at my doorstep so to say. For the first time in my life I became familiar with four, clearly demarcated seasons. People wore different types of clothing during the different seasons. I enjoyed the arrival of autumn, leaves of broad-leafed trees changing colour, and I longed to see a snowfall, but found the damp winter weather very difficult to cope with. The woollen clothes and heavy winter coats were cumbersome and there was always an undesirable smell in churches on a Sunday. I wondered why people did not wash their clothes or get them cleaned. I realised later on that the smell was from the damp coats people wore. Remember not many homes had central heating!

I simply could not wait to welcome the glorious spring. I had heard from my Irish friends that there was no other season like it. I had been taught at length about the 'host of golden daffodils' when I was at school, but had never seen a daffodil. In fact I saw my first daffodil in Max florist shop in Bachelor's Walk. The shop is still there! The joy and excitement of seeing all those bunches of daffodils in buckets of water was indescribable. I had not ventured out very far to look for country gardens. And then one day out of the blue came an invitation from a friend to spend a weekend in County Wexford. It was early spring and I saw fields and fields of daffodils, and came to understand fully the poetic words of William Wordsworth. I spent endless happy hours walking amongst all those daffodils. Over the years, the first snowdrops, crocuses, cherry tree blossoms and many other spring flowering plants continued to delight me, and still do.

How fortunate the Irish people are not to have extremes of weather, I thought, and yet why are they always complaining about the weather? This was never a topic of conversation in the tropics, and I found it fascinating when people here talked so much about it. A lady I met on the road during my first winter here told me, "Oh dear, we won't see the sun for a good number of months, you must find it very difficult to cope with our climate." In my ignorance, I really believed that I would not see the sun and this truly worried me. Would there be no light at all during the winter months? How wrong I was, I saw the sun all right but there was no heat in the sunshine. However, I recall standing at a bus stop one cold winter morning in early December and wondering quietly, "How on earth do people here put up with these dark grey mornings?" What I had not seen was snowfall. "Not yet, perhaps around Christmas," my flatmates had said. True enough snow fell after Christmas that year. I went out just to experience the snow falling, though I was disappointed that it was not heavy. With great joy I wrote to my parents: "Snow fell on me today."

As spring and summer arrived, I was foolish to assume that it would be sunshine all the way. Alas! as I remember, there were more showers than sunshine. Yet, it was great to see people smiling, laughing and sunbathing. My flatmates and all the other tenants in the house were stretched out on every available open space under the warm blue skies. So were the students – male and female bodies everywhere in Trinity College. I found all this very amusing. Here I was, with a tan and not concerned one bit with lying in the sun, and yet all these people were dying for a tan! I simply failed to understand the obsession with having a sun-tan. When I plucked enough courage to ask my friends why they were so keen on getting a tan I was told that the tanned look was much better and, anyway, they enjoyed soaking up the warm sunshine – it was healthy. (There were no health warnings about long hours of sunbathing those days.) I did feel sorry for some people who were really badly burned by the sun – and then all their skin peeling off! Europeans in my own country always wore sensible straw hats or topees to protect themselves from the hot, tropical sun. The natives too, relied on umbrellas or covered their heads with a piece of colourful cloth to get some protection from the hot sun.

Getting used to Irish food took me a while. Irish stew on a very cold day, or a cold salad with mayonnaise from a bottle on a warm evening – neither appealed to my palate, which was so accustomed to the spicy vegetarian food of Ceylon. However, such was the generosity and kindness of a number of the Irish people I had got to know in the short space of time since I arrived in Dublin, that invariably I was invited to Sunday dinners with their families. Sundays were very special for many Irish families. The menu usually consisted of soup, roast pork with crackling or lovely roast beef or spring lamb roast with mint sauce and the delightful home grown Irish potatoes, along with two boiled vegetables. There was always a desert, and sherry trifle seemed to feature a lot. No matter how many roast, boiled, or how much mashed potatoes I consumed, however, I still wanted a bowl of rice.

The Universal Chinese restaurant on Wicklow Street served a full three-course lunch with rice or potato chips for 5s.6d. On a student's monthly allowance of £30, I managed to eat there once a month on a Saturday. Pudding rice was available in the grocers' shops, but I was looking for good quality long grain rice. I did succeed, and the little grocer's shop in Mount Street stocked packets of one pound Roma rice (cost 6d) especially for me and at my request. The Cullen brothers owned that shop, and they were very courteous, kind and always good-humoured. On my way to the flat from college I always went in to the shop to buy a bottle of milk and any other items of food I required. The two brothers made sure to put away some vegetables for me – usually carrots and cabbage in case they were sold out before I arrived from college. Many vegetables, and especially onions, were not available during the winter months, garlic was a luxury too.

Magills, the posh delicatessen shop in Clarendon Street was a little bit of heaven for foreign students in Trinity College and the College of Surgeons. Mr Magill stocked every possible spice from the East and a number of other items such as German sausages, frankfurters, salami, all kinds of cheeses and a large selection of salads which he prepared himself. I was able to buy rice sticks and tins of lychees from Magills in 1967! If there was one man in Ireland who was used to seeing faces from all over the world I can say with confidence it was Mr Magill. The staff who worked behind the counter knew their overseas customers by name and they always had a pleasant word or two for each of them. All the salads for my pre-wedding party were supplied by Magills of Clarendon Street.

Bewleys of Grafton Street was a very special place then and, of course, still is. A wonderful meeting place for the young and not so young. My first cup of coffee in Bewleys cost me a mere 6d! Cherry buns were my favourite. Even if I did not have enough money to go into Bewleys and have a cup of coffee and a bun on a regular basis, it was simply delightful to walk up and down Grafton Street enjoying the aroma of fresh coffee and to take a look in through the window to see the coffee beans being roasted.

Grafton Street was also very special for other reasons. If the coffee aroma of Bewley's welcomed you to this famous street, the fragrance of various brands of perfumes being tested and tried by elegant, and no doubt wealthy ladies in hats and gloves, was synonymous with Brown Thomas – the famous department store. Across the road, there was Switzers, another landmark of Grafton Street. Just like Brown Thomas, Switzers was a spacious and elegant place in which to shop, and I always felt the two stores catered for the wealthy from Dublin and the country. On 8 December, the feast of the Immaculate Conception, the city of Dublin was always unusually crowded, and you could hear many different accents. I came to understand that people from the country simply descended upon the big city to shop! The nuns and the priests came in large numbers too – Wynne's Hotel off Lower Abbey Street was their meeting place.

I wondered often whether Clery's of O'Connell Street served the clothing needs of the religious communities all over Ireland because that is where I saw many nuns.

Arnott's of Henry Street was also an important shopping place for many Dubliners and shoppers from the country. It was always very interesting to walk down O'Connell Street and find all sorts of people – the young and old, the well off and the not so well off, the city, county and country people all gathering around the GPO – another famous meeting place. But of all the streets leading from O'Connell Street, Moore Street off Henry Street, was my favourite place. A street full of ordinary people, and women in particular, selling vegetables, fruit, fish, flowers and all sorts of bits and pieces at a much cheaper price than in the shops or the very few, and not so elaborate, supermarkets.

The street and the vendors boasted a totally different culture from that in the rest of Dublin, and one with which I grew to be familiar. Quickly, I learnt that the people there were in the main from the inner city. It was also evident that people who dwelt in the inner city were not very well off, or for that matter highly educated in the academic sense, but they took a pride in their way of life and making a reasonable living out of their trading on the street. Often I would hear people from the county of Dublin making remarks such as "these people are the salt of the earth" or "they are the real Dubs" and as years went by I grasped the meaning behind such statements. Somehow, the people I came across in Moore Street, be they vendors or buyers always made me feel welcome, found time to quip a few words to me each Saturday afternoon by remembering me from the previous visit I made to buy my vegetables. Simply speaking they all had time, no one was rushing, no one was trying to impress anyone – we were all there because we all had a modest amount of money, and we all did our best to make that money stretch. In the process we provided the much-needed income to the traders but most importantly we were all pleasant to one another. There was no question of anyone being made to feel conscious of their home addresses, the number of pound notes they carried in their purses, or level of education they had. I felt comfortable amongst them all. It never ever occurred to me that I was different in terms of nationality, colour or creed.

There were times I found the accents difficult, the use of English and colloquialisms strange. "Who's yer man?", "Are you doing a line?", "The craic is only ninety", "I'll learn you" or "Cute hoor": *this* language was all very new to me. Very quickly I made the effort to listen carefully, ask for an explanation when

I did not understand what was being said and even use these strange expressions myself. I was a bit puzzled by the phrase 'cute hoor' – what did they mean by 'hoor'? Were they confusing it with 'whore'? Perhaps it was a different way of pronouncing the word – a lady from Kerry managed to explain it to me and quelled my curiosity. The term "your man" gradually crept into my own vocabulary. Just a few months ago a friend of mine pointed out to me that I had used "your man" very casually in a talk I gave to the members of a horticultural society. We both laughed at how very Irish I had become!

Some Irish people found my surname difficult to pronounce – really it would not have been difficult compared with some Irish names and the one I had to try very hard to pronounce was Mac Confhaola. I would write down V-a-l-a-r-a-s-a-n and ask people to try it out phonetically. Easy don't you think? One day in 1968 I had to telephone for a taxi to take me to a friend's wedding. It never felt comfortable or right to dress up in a sari – my national costume – and walk down the street or take a bus. There were times I had no choice and used the public transport. I gave my name to the taxi company as 'Miss Doyle' – because I did not want the voice at the other end of the telephone to say "Who?" or "What?" if I gave my surname as Valarasan. The taxi arrived and the driver rang the doorbell and announced, "Taxi for Miss Doyle." I opened the door and said, "That's me," got into the taxi and gave him the address of my destination. "So, you are Miss Doyle, where did your mother meet the Irishman?" the taxi driver enquired. I knew he would be wondering about my surname. "Oh, in Kildare," I responded. "A rich farmer, eh . . . and you are studying in college I presume. College is only for the rich people in Ireland." If only he knew that I gave my friend Ann's maiden name just to make things easy! Ann and I still laugh about this mischief on my part. Through the years many people managed to pronounce my surname though there are occasions when I have been asked to spell my married name – Toomey. I guess this is because people automatically conclude my name will be difficult to spell. So I prefer to spell it – I wonder whether I should have stuck to Valarasan!

Talking about names, Dunnes and their brand name *St Bernard's* are well known to people in Ireland. Though new on the scene, when I arrived in Dublin, Dunnes Stores has served us well. The one in George's Street was the place to go to and there was an adequate food section – a supermarket of sorts – in addition to the main area, which sold various items of clothing for ladies, gentlemen and children. There were also a number of other smaller and more personal retail clothing outlets as well as grocery shops scattered around the city and county Dublin. Not many Irish households had the luxury of a car, and so the grocers and butchers provided a delivery service to their regular customers. In fact my late mother-in-law had her weekly groceries delivered to her home during the late-1970s and early-1980s. It is good to see the modern supermarkets in Dublin providing a delivery service to those who need it.

Despite the absence of affluence and today's modern conveniences, I noticed that people were generally cheerful and those who were in employment took pride in their work. I was struck by the readiness with which people from all walks of life exchanged greetings or found time to say a few words to each other, or made it a point to call on each other. There was no rush, no pressure, no strain or stress.

I have felt happy to live among Irish people who have exuded warmth, friendship and generosity towards me – an outsider. Here was Christianity working at its best, I thought. I looked forward to going to Church on Sundays; it was always packed with worshippers – women, men, children and teenagers. All of them, and women in particular, were neatly groomed and looked smart in their 'Sunday best' outfits, hats and gloves. The women and girls who did not wear hats always covered their heads with mantillas and one never failed to notice the rosary beads in their hands too. There appeared to be a seriousness of purpose in going to Church then. I was told it was a sin to miss Sunday mass. Therefore, no matter what, people who were Catholics made it a point to arrive in large numbers for one of the many masses said in Latin on a Sunday. It seemed to me neither the children nor the teenagers ever made any fuss about going to church.

The priests, Bishops, Archbishops, Cardinals and the Pope were held in high esteem. I remember the mother of one of my friends inviting the parish priest to afternoon tea, she spent the whole morning cleaning and dusting the house, polishing her brass and silver, and taking every care to set the table immaculately hours before he arrived. There seemed to be a much revered, ceremonial approach to welcoming the priest for a cup of tea. I was amazed at the esteem in which the parish priest was held, and by all accounts the priest enjoyed not only the splendid baking of the lady but also the respect and kindness bestowed upon him. At all times the priest was addressed with the title "Father". Equally, the reverend sisters accorded the priests who visited the convents the very best of welcomes and hospitality. I really believed that a priest's job was most exciting and rewarding – he could do no wrong, he was an extraordinary human being, almost next to the Lord Himself.

By contrast, the Catholic priests and nuns in my own native land seemed to live a very quiet life. All I could remember as a child attending the convent school in Ceylon was the priests in white robes and brown sandals on ladies' bicycles going about their business. They were not really anything special. I guess that was because Ceylon was a multi-religious country with Buddhism being the most predominant religion. Ireland being mainly Catholic was very preoccupied with its religion and an enormous amount of time, energy and money were given over to the Church. No-one seemed to question the words of the Church or the priests.

A great emphasis was placed on the word 'sin'. I was taken aback by the children in primary schools being so aware of this word. Preparation for making their first Holy Communion involved doing absolutely nothing sinful for fear of not being allowed to take part in the whole process if they inadvertently told a lie or stole a biscuit or a sweet, even in their own homes. I distinctly remember a young child attending a second-level school telling me that she was afraid to go to mass on a Sunday and receive Holy Communion without going to confession simply because she told a lie to her mother and that was a sin. Despite all the fears, adults and the young seemed to practise their religion faithfully – at least that is how it appeared to me.

Since there was a ban on Catholics attending Trinity College, most of the students and staff there were Protestants. However, there were a few Irish-Catholic students who had received dispensation from the then Archbishop of Dublin, Dr Charles McQuaid, to attend the College. I was somewhat puzzled by this ban on Catholics attending an internationally well-known college in their own land and in the heart of Dublin. Being pre-occupied with my studies I really did not bother to find out the reasons for the ban.

It was interesting to observe that there was very little communication between the Catholics and Protestants. Strangely enough I knew instinctively who was a Protestant and who was a Catholic when I met people in academic and social gatherings. In fact the two groups of people spoke somewhat differently, and their accents were different. It appeared to me that the Protestants were somewhat reserved, and their sense of humour not as obvious as that of the Catholics. I also learnt that there were individuals in the Protestant community who owned a number of big businesses and big properties, and had more disposable income. Their children, in the main, attended exclusive, second-level, Protestant schools. Those who wished to pursue third-level education almost always enrolled in Trinity College. Those who wanted to train as primary school teachers attended the Church of Ireland Training College.

During my student days at Trinity there were also a number of Protestant students from Northern Ireland and quite a few from Great Britain as well. The college also attracted students from Asia, Africa and America and most overseas students who wished to follow a course in medicine arrived in the Royal College of Surgeons in Dublin. My family's GP in Ceylon was an old student of the Royal College of Surgeons and he always talked at length about his student days in Dublin every time I visited his surgery during my childhood.

However, not many foreigners came to live and work here. The few who came especially from the Indian sub-continent, Singapore, Malaysia and few African countries were medical doctors who worked in the hospitals as registrars and at the same time studied for their post-graduate qualifications. One or two of these professional people also married Irish nationals and took up residence here.

To the best of my knowledge there was no major problem for any foreigner including myself to live here permanently. I remember going to Dublin Castle and having my passport stamped by an official – it simply stated that I could stay in Ireland indefinitely which of course I have, as I married an Irishman. At the time I graduated there was a dearth of well-qualified science teachers/lecturers and a few of us from Trinity College gained employment in third-level establishments. In essence, the Ireland into which I came 30 years ago had no difficulty in accepting foreigners, irrespective of nationality, colour or creed into their communities, and there was no official red tape either. However, one must appreciate very few foreigners chose to arrive here as immigrants and they did not seek any financial help from the Irish Government. In short there were no economic immigrants.

The Irish themselves emigrated to many parts of the world in search of skilled and unskilled jobs. Quite a number of Irish graduates also went to some African countries such as Kenya, Nigeria, Ghana and Zambia to serve as lay teachers in many Catholic schools. During my brief teaching days in Nigeria I also met a number of Irish nurses, doctors, teachers and engineers working there as lay missionaries or volunteers on limited salaries. There was no doubt the Irish on the whole were at ease with different nationalities be it in their own land or abroad. The fact that Ireland up to the early 1960s was not a wealthy nation did not seem to matter.

As I remember, Irish people went about making meaningful and rewarding lives for themselves and the community in which they lived. People gave of their time to raise funds for worthy causes, be they in Ireland or in the developing nations. I was struck by the phenomenal amount of work done by religious people for schools, hospitals and for the homeless and the poor. I concluded that the education, health and some social services of this small nation depended largely on religious communities. Many of the religious people who went abroad and to Africa in particular, tirelessly spread the good news of not only Christ and Christianity, or more precisely Catholicism, but also that Ireland was a land of the thousand welcomes!

The one abiding memory of my very early years in Dublin was an innocent statement made by a child to her mother at a bus stop in Burgh Quay. "Mummy, Why is this lady all dressed up in a long skirt? Is she waiting to take a bus to the church to get married?" The child was referring to my white sari – most probably she and her mother had never seen anyone in a sari before. I would love to have known what the mother said to the child about my clothes.

Chapter 2

1970–1980: the decade of disillusionment

Thanks to the friendliness of the Dubliners, I felt that I had, well and truly, become a part of the Irish society. By the early-1970s, I had made many friends, and felt at home. As a minority citizen in the land I was born, I knew there was no future for me there. People like me from many parts of the world who are treated as second-class citizens in their own native countries or elsewhere, either learn to accept that we will always be victims of discrimination or become a sort of a 'nomad' hoping after hope, that some day, somewhere, we will be treated as equals and with dignity. I had found such a place in Dublin, and I saw no reason to uproot myself and leave Ireland though I had the opportunity to live and work elsewhere.

At the beginning of the 1970s, there was a shortage of teachers to teach the newly-introduced subject of biology in the Leaving Certificate curriculum. I was recruited by the Department of Education to give teachers' courses in biology at various centres throughout the country. This gave me confidence in my ability as a teacher, and also an opportunity to travel around Ireland and see the countryside, meet people outside Dublin and enjoy their hospitality and kindness.

There I was, one summer in the Dingle Peninsula having taken a weekend break from a teachers' course I was giving in Tralee, showing children who be-friended me how to make and fly a kite. Kite-flying was a great pastime during my childhood in Jaffna and I considered myself to be an expert. I had great fun with the children in Dingle. The local people seemed to be very impressed with my kite-flying abilities, and my friendly attitude towards them and the children. A publican invited me to his pub "to have a few drinks with the locals". Without any inhibition, I accepted his invitation, and had an enjoyable Saturday evening. My belief that I belonged in Ireland was reinforced after my trip to the Dingle Peninsula, miles and miles away from the heart of Dublin and Trinity College.

Therefore, I stopped wondering about where the next port of call in my life would be and settled down to a life in Ireland. For the first time in my life I felt confident to be part of a nation, and to be a contributor. All credit for this must go to the Irish people, from all walks of life, that I met and got to know, and who gave me every encouragement to become actively involved in Irish life. The officials in the Department of Education had absolutely no difficulty in recognising, utilising and rewarding my intellectual ability. The Educational Company of Ireland, on the recommendation of many science teachers I taught, commissioned me to write a book on biology for schools, and I had also been recruited as a lecturer in the newly opened Regional Technical College in Dundalk. A very generous lady outside Dundalk gave me comfortable accommodation. She enjoyed calling me a faggot – I never knew why. When I decided to buy a small house in Dundalk, the Educational Building Society readily gave me a mortgage. The interesting point is no-one ever bothered to question my status as a single woman, or a legal immigrant. I knew I had an endorsement in my passport to say that I could live here legally and without "condition to time" which meant that I could stay as long as I wished. They all just accepted me as a person, which was very important for me.

I also met my future husband and got married in 1973, much against the wishes of my parents, and my mother in particular. Soon afterwards I applied for Irish citizenship and the Department of Justice dealt with my application very quickly and positively. I remember with great pride the day I became an Irish citizen. One of my husband's late aunts and her husband who lived in Clontarf, and who were extremely kind to me from the very day we met and welcomed me into their family, took time off from their work to celebrate the occasion of me becoming a citizen of their country. "Ceylon's loss is our gain," was the toast that evening. I was so touched by their generous gesture that I wrote at length to my father and mother to say how very fortunate I was to live in the 'land of thousand welcomes'. Any wonder then, as a citizen I took enormous interest in Ireland and felt very involved. I was keen to learn as much as I could about my new country, the people, places, politics, politicians, political parties, history, education and native flora and fauna. When I talked to a number of people in Cork to get an insight into how they viewed the phenomenal changes in Ireland during the past few years, one gentleman quipped, "My word, for someone who came to live amongst us, you certainly have a wonderful grasp of all things Irish." I felt very flattered.

Looking back, I view the decade of the 1970s as a very important one in the history of Ireland. On 6 May 1970, the then Taoiseach Jack Lynch dismissed C J Haughey, Minister for Finance, Neil T Blaney, Minister for Agriculture and Kevin Boland,

Minister for Local Government and towards the end of the month the first two were charged with conspiring to import, illegally, arms and ammunition into the country. Almost everyone I knew discussed Charles Haughey at length, they held a sort of 'love-hate' attitude towards him, his politics and political activities. I was amazed at the level of political awareness, understanding and comprehension of political matters by the Irish people compared with other nationalities I knew. It is certainly not necessary to be highly educated in political science to understand and appreciate politics and government. The Irish people are masters of politics, and no-one should ever underestimate their grasp and understanding of political matters. The more I discussed party politics with my friends, the more I became apprehensive about Fianna Fail, though I had great admiration for Jack Lynch and the late George Colley. How right George Colley was, when he talked about "low standards in high places". Now I know what he really meant and why he made that allusion about some people who held very high political positions in this nation.

As someone always interested in politics, I joined the Fine Gael party. I believe that this was due to my admiration of Dr Garret Fitzgerald, his intellect and eloquence. He always struck me as an extremely honest person and lacked the 'cuteness' of other politicians in Ireland. While I am very interested in political matters, not for a moment did I wish to become a politician. I strongly believe that a number of good citizens who enter politics commence their political life highly motivated by ideals and a deep desire to contribute their best, but once they are in, they become engulfed by the political system and power – ask a politician a question, and seldom are you given a straightforward answer. This seems to be universally true and not just an Irish phenomenon. I remember Michael D Higgins of the Labour Party, once he became a Minister often finding himself in situations where his words failed to flow freely, especially when confronted with questions about his Government's policies. Yet he was very eloquent when he sat on the opposition benches – for a very long time too. I had the pleasure of meeting him with a group of Galway graduates in a pub around 1972, and I was very impressed with his idealism.

The 1970s also saw the power of the Catholic Church weaken albeit slowly, and that of Irish women strengthen. The Catholic Church's gradual loss of power and influence began in June 1970, with the announcement by the hierarchy removing its restrictions on Catholics attending Trinity College. Almost a year later, members of the Irish Women's Liberation Movement challenged the Church's attitude and teaching with regard to contraceptives, and defied the law of the country by importing contraceptives from Belfast. Though I realised that in quite a number of areas women were discriminated against by the State and the Church, I did not have the courage or confidence to join the Women's Liberation Movement and to lend my support. I believed that as a foreigner it would be wrong to do so. My Irish friends, both male and female were excited about what was taking place in their country and discussed with me the urgent need for changes in the laws, specifically with regard to women. They explained their views to me that the Catholic Church had too much influence on the affairs of the State. They felt confident that sooner or later the Catholic Church and the State would not be so intricately linked, especially with the country awaiting its entry into the EEC.

Nevertheless I was taken aback when, in the referendum held in December 1972, people voted for the deletion from the Irish Constitution of reference to the special position of the Catholic Church. I did not think that my friends' prediction would come true so quickly. Yet I knew that long before I arrived in Dublin, the Church had dominated affairs of the State. I had also witnessed the end of Dr John Charles McQuaid's reign of power and influence and now realised that most probably people had had enough of living under that dominance. Ireland was ready to leave the past, examine and analyse the present, and have the courage to embrace the future. Naturally we had to learn to walk before we could run and perhaps a small but not insignificant sign of change was the decimalization of the currency. The older generation definitely found this difficult but gradually accepted and adjusted to the fact that change was the order of the day.

The future lay in Europe and Ireland became a member of the EEC in January 1973. She began to move away from a primarily agricultural economy towards a manufacturing one. Multi-national electronic, chemical and pharmaceutical companies arrived on the scene and the prospects for employment improved. The first batch of young graduates from the new Regional Technical Colleges were able to find jobs very quickly in their chosen areas. Some highly educated and experienced Irish emigrants returned to live and work here, although more were leaving than returning. There was a new-found optimism and confidence, a feeling of self-sufficiency and an air of happiness everywhere. Irish women felt they too were embarking on a new era, because in February 1973, a few weeks after Ireland's entry into the EEC, the Report of the Commission on

Status of Women was published. This recommended equal pay, maternity leave, day-care for children, marriage counselling, family-planning advice and an end to sexual discrimination in employment. The clear message was that, "we are all Europeans and we not going to be a small island on the perimeter of Western Europe dictated to by the Catholic Church".

Unfortunately, this feeling of euphoria was short-lived because as Ireland joined the EEC, the oil crisis started to cause havoc all over the world. Petrol was not readily available and there were large queues at the petrol stations. It appeared that the economies of Europe and the rest of the world were being dictated to by the oil-rich Middle Eastern countries. Suddenly terms such as inflation, recession, high interest rates, shorter working weeks and redundancies became household phrases. There were many strikes, the trade unions became vociferous and dissatisfaction was rife. The cost of living and interest rates kept soaring. The property market became sluggish, mortgages were not easily available, and the building sector suffered. Unemployment was a major item on the political agenda with the Government struggling to cope with this problem. Once again emigration in search of jobs and better lives became the norm – there was an air of doom and gloom. If it had not been for the inflow of money into the economy following Ireland's entry into the EEC, the country would have been much more severely damaged by the 1973 recession and its aftermath. There was no doubt Irish membership of the EEC brought many economic benefits and changes to Ireland, a small country which up to joining the EEC had been to a large extent dependent on, and even dominated by, trade with Great Britain.

It took me a very long time to understand the ambivalent attitude of some Irish people towards the British and English people in particular. A large number of Irish people lived and worked in England. More and more people were emigrating to England in search of jobs and quite a number of English people lived in Ireland as well. I had also met quite a few English students and staff in Trinity College. What was the problem between the Irish and the English?

Ceylon was governed by the British too, but as I understood from my father, the minority Tamil people enjoyed many privileges during the British rule. Soon after the independence from the British, 50 years ago, the Tamils lost all these advantages and became second-class citizens. Therefore, I can only say that I personally have no bitter memories about the British rule of my native land. For that matter, despite all the injustices, civil war, 40,000 deaths, mostly young men and women during the past fifteen years, the personal suffering of my family and people – many finding themselves in refugee camps, seeking asylum in other countries – I remain optimistic, and without any hatred towards the majority Sinhalese people, that one day peace and harmony will return to my small island, the pearl of the Indian Ocean. My one and only fervent hope and prayer is that no matter what, Ceylon should not be partitioned. That would spell disaster. If there is something my people who are fighting for a separate nation can learn from Northern Ireland, it is to look at the consequences of dividing one island into two separate parts.

The events that took place during the early-1970s in Northern Ireland left me frightened and very concerned for the whole of Ireland. One particular event in November 1971 made an indelible impression on me. Three women from the Bogside area of Derry were 'tarred and feathered' for 'fraternising' with young British soldiers. Without realising the support that the IRA had from a family with whom I was friendly, I expressed my revulsion at the mutilations caused to these women, during a dinner party in their house. I remember being politely but firmly told that I had no business to comment on the incident or express my views on Ireland. Yet there was a universal disgust and outcry about the manner in which the heads of women were shorn and daubed with red paint and tar. I became cautious after being criticised for my comments at the dinner party and refrained from discussing Northern Ireland with anyone – be they friends, neighbours or acquaintances.

Though I agonised within when I saw the news on television about the shootings by British paratroopers in Derry's Bogside area, which killed thirteen people on 30 January 1972, I only wrote about 'Bloody Sunday', to my father. I just did not have the courage to make any comments to anyone in Ireland or England. There were more horrendous bombings, shootings, deaths, destruction and injustices in Northern Ireland and Britain throughout the 1970s. RTÉ radio and television and the newspapers kept me informed, I even wondered at times what would the media talk and write about if peace and harmony were restored to Northern Ireland.

Away from all the troubles in Northern Ireland, the Republic was doing its best to solve the unemployment problem and improve its economy. In 1977 Fianna Fail won the election by a very large majority and what I called a 'goodies package' came with that victory. The ordinary citizen obviously was delighted that he or she did not have to pay rates and road tax. What the people did not realise was the nation was on the road to incurring a massive debt as a result of the policies adopted by this government. Income tax became a huge burden especially on the PAYE sector. There were different levies imposed not only to fund the essential needs of the country but also to service the national debt. Life was difficult for everyone and the take-home pay of those who were in employment did not seem as good as it should have been. People had to work very hard to make ends meet. A sense of insecurity set in, those who worked in the private sector in particular were gripped with the fear of redundancies.

Despite the economic difficulties coupled with rising unemployment and high income taxes, I recall 1979 with great joy and sadness. On 9 August 1979 Ireland opened her doors and welcomed 59 Vietnamese refugees – the 'Boat People'. However small the number of refugees was, taking into account there were so many displaced Vietnamese people as a result of the war in Vietnam, I rejoiced at their safe arrival in Dublin. I heard no-one accusing the refugees of taking their homes and jobs or living off social welfare. To the best of my memory the Minister for Justice at that time did not scream about how many thousands of pounds these refugees would cost the Government so frightening the native Irish population. On the contrary, the Vietnamese refugees were given every help to integrate into the Irish community.

The reason for my sadness was the IRA bomb that killed Lord Mountbatten in Mullaghmore, County Sligo on 29 August. Lord Mountbatten had served as the last Viceroy of India and was someone I held in high esteem. I was horrified and all I could do was to sit down and write a lengthy letter to my infant daughter, Aoife, about the futility of that murder in the hope that she would read it one day in the future, when she was old enough to understand the history of Ireland. I said to her:

> Perhaps by the time you read this letter, the two communities in Northern Ireland, the Irish and British Governments would have found a solution to the Northern Ireland problem. The IRA cannot, and will not, unite Ireland with bombs. Compromise, Consent and Co-operation – the three Cs are essential for Peace, Prosperity and Pluralism – the 3 Ps in this island.

The 1970s was by no means an easy decade for many people, not only in Ireland but all over the world. The 1960s when I was a young adult belonged to the 'youth culture' and 'flower power'. The 'idealistic' young people truly believed that they could transform the world. The 1970s however witnessed the rise and rise of international terrorism, economic instability and industrial unrest. Ireland shed the protective mantle of the Church, adapted to her new role and exerted her new-found confidence into the 1980s.

Chapter 3

1980–1990: the decade of despair and hope

If the 1970s were about oil price wars, industrial unrest, economic decline, high unemployment and international terrorism – all of which affected, directly or indirectly, our small nation – then the early 1980s did not bring any major changes about which we could rejoice. However, in the summer of 1981, Dr Garret Fitzgerald became Taoiseach. Perhaps more importantly and in spite of all the anti-Royal feelings expressed by some Irish people, almost all Irish eyes watched, on their televisions, the pageantry of the wedding of the Prince of Wales and Lady Diana Spencer. Anyone and everyone I knew discussed the beauty of Princess Diana and were very happy for her and Prince Charles. I must say the Irish people have an innate capacity to enjoy the good things in life even during hard times. They can talk and laugh about people they have never met as if those people are their personal friends. Equally they can be critical about strangers they have never met.

I received a taste of how critical and vociferous some Irish people can become over certain matters in 1983. I remember it as a very difficult and controversial year: the year of the 'Pro-Life' referendum. Many people chose to refer to it as the 'Abortion' Referendum. I found it difficult to discuss any aspect of this referendum with anyone. One incident that I found difficult to explain or understand during the height of heated discussions and debate about the pros and cons of the referendum, was a phone call I had from the County Council, asking me whether I was an Irish citizen. Perhaps someone was anxious that I should or should not vote. I even wondered did someone really take the trouble to check the fact of my citizenship and my right to vote? This is in itself a good thing and gives an indication of how aware and informed the people are about important issues that deeply concern them. However, on 7 September 1983, the 'Pro-Life' amendment to the Constitution was carried by 841,233 votes to 416,136.

While people were debating and discussing the 'Pro-Life' referendum, the nation was faced with the problems of factory closures, unemployment and redundancies. Gay Byrne kept screaming about the economic state of the country on his daily radio programme and advised the people to emigrate in search of better lives. Joy-riders and car thefts in Dublin were an added headache too. I could not help noticing the social fabric of the society in which we lived coming apart at the seams. The explanation from the pundits on politics and economics was conveyed in a solitary word – recession.

It had never occurred to me that educated people in work would suddenly find themselves unemployed. I recalled the words of my father, a principal of a high school in Ceylon, "Sound education is a passport to secure life." I wished it was true as we were faced with redundancy. It was 1984 and it was December – with Christmas just around the corner. No doubt there were many who found themselves in the same situation as we did and everyone who became redundant was frantically looking for a job in different parts of Ireland. Reluctantly, we moved to Scotland in January 1985, my husband having found a job in Glasgow. I remember a friend of mine praising the perspicacity of the Scots at that time. But, I was shattered at the very thought of having to leave Dublin and Ireland where I had lived so happily for eighteen years and where I had enjoyed a sense of identity and belonging.

To leave my home, my adopted land, my friends and my neighbours who had shared in our happiness, our success and also seen us through difficult and sad times over a number of years, was extremely difficult. I worried intensely about many things: the fear of the unknown destination, the loss of my personal identity in a strange city and, how an Irish-Ceylonese family would be accepted by the people of Glasgow. In all the years I have lived and worked in Dublin and Dundalk, I had never experienced any major difficulties on a personal or professional level. Even as a full-time mother at home I was very involved with voluntary, community work, I enjoyed organising summer civic projects for the youth in the community, planting trees and shrubs in open areas – encouraging people to take care of their gardens, of the environment to make it a pleasant one for all of us living in the area. The very thought of moving away from a society which had given me a purposeful and productive life simply crushed all my confidence. Children always adjust to new environments much better than their parents. I knew our only child and daughter would have no problems making that move from Dublin to Glasgow and as it turned out I was right.

In May 1985, as we were getting organised to leave for Scotland, I became very perturbed about my own native land, Ceylon. Tamil violence had begun to spread and I feared for the safety and welfare of my parents. There was very little I could do from Dublin and yet I longed to run back to my hometown and reason with the young men and women in my community. I had seen the disastrous and painful effects of continuing violence in Northern Ireland. I just did not want my own people – the Tamils – or the Sinhalese, to suffer. I just hoped that the political and religious leaders of the two communities would get together and talk their way towards a peaceful settlement. With that hope I packed our bags and we left for Glasgow.

The eighteen months I spent in Glasgow were not particularly happy ones for me. I could not settle down, and for the first time in my life I was homesick. Homesick for Dublin, homesick for my friends, neighbours and acquaintances. I missed the laughter, the humour of the Irish people, the friendliness of people in supermarkets and the streets; I even missed the Irish weather as strange as that may sound. No, Dublin skies were never that grey. Winter was never that severe. In fact the winter of 1984-85 had been an unusually cold one in Ireland, and I had been delighted to see so much snow in Dublin. Even without any snow, Glasgow to me was very depressing. I found the Glaswegian accent difficult to understand, the acres of rundown flats in Springburn were most distressing as I drove past them towards the city, I did not know anyone to visit or even to phone and have a chat with. The Irish spoiled me and suddenly, here I was in a new place not knowing how to cope.

I wrote to my friends and acquaintances, I telephoned them just to hear the Irish voice and enjoy their humour and laughter. No matter what I did, I just became more and more miserable. I longed to return home to Ireland. I missed all the news on the Irish national radio, reading *The Irish Times*, though I managed to have a copy of Saturday's *Irish Times* posted out to me. I read it from cover to cover and managed to keep in touch with what was happening in Ireland. Such was my passion for my adopted nation. One day a letter arrived from a friend of mine, a Holy Ghost Father: "You are obviously suffering from a culture shock, you must make every effort to return to Dublin where I know you will be yourself and be happy." He was right, but we had to wait for an opportune moment to make that journey back home.

All through my months in Glasgow, I wrote at length to one or two friends. This helped me to ventilate my sadness and frustration and also cope with loneliness.

9 July 1985
Glasgow

Dear . . .

Well, another port of call in my nomadic life. Is it the price one pays for being an emigrant? Is that what happens to people who have no roots? It was no fault of mine that I was born into the minority community in my own land. At least I felt I belonged somewhere when I lived in Dublin and now I am nobody in a strange neighbourhood. As a student in the heart of Dublin, life was just wonderful. Grafton Street, Bewleys – beautiful mugs of coffee plus all those endless chats with my pals – but the important thing is there was so much space and not crowds and crowds of people in Dublin – surely I am not imagining. Here, the city is so crowded. It is just like a week before Christmas in Dublin city centre. I guess if all the Irish did not emigrate Dublin would be full of people too! Sooner or later I will have to return to Dublin or I will go mad.

Yours etc.

---

15 July 1985
Glasgow

Dear . . .

I am just miserable. I miss Dublin, my very own home for nearly eighteen years! The facilities are just great here. The roads are swept regularly and I have not seen any sign of litter in the suburb where we live. I am sure if Ireland had more money we too would have clean roads and more litter bins, and perhaps no litter. There are hanging baskets, barrels of plants and flowers to delight people on the roads with the compliments of Strathkelvin District Council. Just imagine the bin men walk right down to the back garden, collect the rubbish bags, and leave two clean bags for the following week. Why two bags – one for the domestic refuse and the other for the garden refuse. Well I never! All this is alien to me – looking back I was happy with the litter and no free litter bags. I would rather be in Dublin. You know how I love Dublin.

Ireland is very special, the people gave me a sense of belonging and identity which I never knew in my own land of birth. I had a very successful academic career all thanks to good old Ireland! She will always be the jewel in my crown. By the way, some of my neighbours spend hours and hours on a Sunday washing their cars – we seem to be the only family that goes to church on Sundays. I guess someone has to say the prayers! There are very few people in the church we go to, but there appears to be a seriousness of purpose – a lot of singing too. I like that.

Yours etc.,

---

30 April 1986
Glasgow

Dear . . .

Very sad about Mrs Jennifer Guinness being kidnapped. I hope no harm will come to her. The BBC showed a good bit of the suburbs of Dublin. Some of the people in our neighbourhood were very surprised to see that there are some fabulous houses there. Some even commented on how articulate the Irish were – strange they think we are still a backward nation. What is Bord Fáilte doing I wonder? There is so much to show off about our country. I enjoyed Mrs Guinness's sense of humour. She simply repeated what the kidnappers said to her "Jesus missus, you are worth millions." Oh! how I miss the Irish sense of humour. Our English neighbours are most helpful especially when it comes to gardening and plants. Believe it or not they still have not met Barry. The English gentleman keeps running in every time I want to introduce Barry to him. I wonder why! No sense of humour though – very serious.

Yours etc.,

---

22 October 1986
Glasgow

Dear . . .

Good news. The emigrants are returning home. Perhaps not with a big bank balance but more than happy to arrive home and pay the high income tax in Ireland. I have no qualms paying for that very special quality of Irish life I enjoyed for eighteen years. I am more Irish than the Irish themselves – fancy this brown, Irishwoman giving out yards about this or that. I know Ireland is not a rich country but I tell you she will be very soon. Surely the time is fast approaching for Ireland to enjoy the benefits of the European membership. I only hope we will not lose the quality of Irish life if we ever become affluent. The Irish welcome with smiles, chats and humour – very important to hold on to them. They are their major assets – money or no money. Can't wait for that cup of coffee in Bewleys!

I only hope Ireland did not suffer too much from the Chernobyl disaster. There is so much talk about the radioactive fall-out. I was too scared to write about this awful nuclear accident to you. I fear for the future. I was very deeply concerned for the welfare of our child and all other children, adults and the environment after we were told the facts about the accident at the Chernobyl nuclear power station. It was only after high radiation levels were detected in Sweden that the gravity of the situation arising out of the radioactive fall-out came to light. It was too late, we had consumed radioactive meat, vegetables and milk – the warning not to eat those foodstuffs did not come in time. As a biologist, I know there will be disastrous consequences arising out of the Chernobyl disaster in years to come. Much of Europe was contaminated by the radioactive fall-out and so, parts of Ireland could not have escaped. Time will tell!

Yours etc.,

We returned home in December 1986. Ireland looked good and there was a 'feel-good factor' among the people I met. The young were oozing with confidence. I could not understand why the media, and radio in particular, painted a negative image of Ireland when I was living abroad. On arrival in Dublin, I could not help thinking that the benefits of the European membership had given rise to better national roads, better standards of living, better lifestyle, better shopping complexes and improved leisure facilities. I noticed a greater emphasis on healthier living. The diversity and ready availability of international foods in the supermarkets gave an indication of the changing food habits and preferences of the Irish people. The 1980s were considered to be the decade of plentiful, good food and certainly Ireland was there with all its own culinary delights. The weekend supplements of the national newspapers placed a great emphasis on food, leisure and now a new fashion was beginning to grip the nation and Dublin in particular – gardening.

Gurus of food and gardening were plenty. This was not the Ireland I knew in the 1970s. The property market had picked up and new houses were being built everywhere. Above all I observed a greater emphasis on third-level education. The introduction of free second-level education in the late 1960s had begun to show results. The realisation that higher education is a good passport to employment seemed to have dawned on the Irish people. Christina Murphy, the late education correspondent of *The Irish Times* promoted the various opportunities available to the second-level school students taking the Leaving Certificate Examination via her writings. So, Ireland was wide-awake, full of vim, vigour, vitality and vision, ready to take on the challenges of the 1990s.

While I rejoiced about the Irish progress, a part of me was aching for peace in my own native land. A friend of mine, a religious sister who ran a large convent and many orphanages wrote to me about the plight of Tamil refugees. The refugee camps were bursting at the seams; there was an urgent need for food, blankets, clothing and other basic essentials. She was doing her best with her community of religious sisters but needed financial help. The least I could do from a distance was to raise funds in Dublin. I was even prepared to seek some financial aid from the Irish Government to alleviate the hardships of my own people, including my parents. I approached two politicians I knew well to highlight the plight of the Tamil refugees. They were most sympathetic and assured me that they would raise the issue of the Tamil refugees in the Dáil, and do whatever they could for me and my own people back in my homeland. It was the summer of 1988. I was determined to galvanise all my efforts, and ask my friends, acquaintances and local churches and schools to help me raise funds for a very worthy cause. I knew the Irish people, as always, would rise to the occasion and help out the needy and they did with great sincerity. Once again I felt very proud of the community in which I lived and belonged.

My local Church of Ireland rector and his wife were extremely helpful and with the help of their own congregation organised a bridge session and delivered a handsome cheque to Trocaire. While my friends in various parts of Dublin and the rest of the country were busy organising numerous functions to raise funds, the Methodist Church in Dún Laoghaire gave me the opportunity to address its congregation about the Tamil refugee problem and why urgent funds were needed. The Methodist Church is very strong in many parts of Ceylon. My mother went to a large Methodist school in my town, my three sisters were all educated by the Methodists, and I went to a Methodist primary school. Just a week before I was due to talk in the Methodist Church, I received a letter written by my mother, and sent via a Tamil refugee who had arrived in London asking me to send boxes of matches – there was no electricity – and some medicine for her eczema, which was causing her great pain and discomfort.

When I arrived at the Methodist Church, I brought with me a box of matches to show the congregation and made an appeal to donate whatever they could for the Tamil refugees. I requested the Minister of the Church to send the donation to Oxfam – an organisation that has always been very close to my heart – which worked in India and Ceylon. Monies raised by all my friends were sent to my friend, the Reverend Mother Superior of the convent, who had first alerted me to the plight of the Tamil refugees. The generosity of the Irish people towards my own people was unbelievable – my original nationality, my immigrant status and my colour simply had no bearing on what they wished to do for a community of refugees so far away. People just wanted to help. They responded promptly, with a deep sense of urgency to my appeal on behalf of the Tamil refugees in Ceylon.

Chapter 4

Family

What is a family? This word has many definitions which vary in different parts of the world. In the Ireland to which I came in the late-1960s a typical Irish-Catholic family was a large one, while a Protestant one was small with two or three children. The Catholic family consisted of a set of parents, their children and possibly the maternal and paternal grandparents. It would also be right to define the typical Irish family as one that prayed together and stayed together. The nuclear family was all-important both in Dublin and the rest of the island. It was very much the sense of family that I was used to in my own land. The father was the head of the family and the mother was the homemaker. Women in the 1960s did not appear to worry about a routine question, which featured as a matter of course in the census forms, "Who is the head of the family?" Not many married women who had a family went out to work. They could not have done so because it was not socially acceptable for a woman to continue working once she got married. Legally – until a change in the law in 1973 – she had to resign if her job was in the public service.

Most families in Ireland were by global (and in particular Western) standards, big because of the number of children. Good Catholic people by virtue of their Church's teachings on family did not resort to any form of artificial methods of family planning. Contraceptives were not there, even if some wished to limit the number of children. When a young man showed me his wedding photograph taken with his family in 1988 he proudly proclaimed "you can see I have fifteen brothers and sisters, thank God they are all alive and well even though not all of them live in Ireland right now". My immediate question was, "How many potatoes did your poor mother have to peel for the dinner when you were all at home?" Just imagine the amount of time that mother would have spent bringing up all those children especially at a time when fathers did not play a great role in domestic matters. Consider the time spent cooking, washing and ironing clothes – at a time when not many households had electrical appliances to reduce the sheer volume of essential manual work involved in caring for a family. Did the woman, the mother, have time for herself? Yet, talking to a number of women during my early years in Ireland, I got the distinct impression that they were thankful to the Lord for blessing them with children. Despite high unemployment and shortage of money, there seemed to be certain contentment in bringing forth children and taking care of them.

The influence of the Catholic Church on family life in Ireland was unquestionably strong. Therefore, the family values were based very much on the teachings of the Church. Sexual matters were never openly discussed, sex within marriage was looked upon only as a requisite to procreation and not for pleasure. There was an apparent reluctance to accept the normal human emotions culminating in sexual activities within marriage because the word sin dominated the lives of many people. Women felt the need to go to confession not only to ask for forgiveness if they had in any way strayed from the teachings of the Church in relation to their sexuality, but also to seek advice from the priest on matters pertaining to their family and family planning.

An acquaintance of mine – a nurse from a country town about an hour's drive from Dublin – explained, "Oh God yes, we relied very much on the priest to guide us and I remember my doctor advising me not to have one child after another because my health was not up to it. So I went to the priest to discuss the problem and ask what I should do. He replied calmly I must always bear in mind my marital duties," she added, "I knew what he was saying and I was so angry that he did not think of me – the woman, the person – and my health." She assured me that many Irish women all over the country were afraid to think of contraception and in her words "even though the famous 'pill' and other types of contraceptives were readily available to women in many developed nations of the world to take control of their lives, Irish women were still waiting – thanks to a State so dominated by the Catholic Church". Contraception was legally available in Ireland as a 'cycle regulator' but because of the unavailability of other forms of contraceptives, women had no choice at all. Even the pill was only available on a medical prescription.

Not all Irish women were prepared to accept the teaching of the Church with regard to contraception or the law, which made the importation of contraceptives an offence. Forty-seven members of the Irish Women's Liberation Movement decided to defy the law by importing contraceptives from Belfast.

"The order came: 'Loose your contraceptives!' and a shower of condoms, pills and spermicidal jelly fell at the feet of customs men and slid along the railway platform towards the waiting crowd. The scene was Connolly station, in Dublin, on Saturday, and members of the Irish Women's Liberation Movement had just returned from Belfast." (*The Irish Times*, 23 May 1971.)

22 May 1971 saw the first public defiance of the law against the importation of contraceptives. The Bishop of Clonfert, the Most Rev Dr Ryan speaking at Knock shrine, County Mayo the following day said that probably never before, certainly not since the penal days, was the Catholic heritage of this country subjected to so many insidious onslaughts on the pretext of conscience, civil rights and women's liberation. The Catholic Church was in for more shocks. Two and a half years later on 19 December 1973, the Supreme Court decided by a majority of four-to-one that the ban on the importation of contraceptives for private use was unconstitutional. The effect of the decision was immediate and the sub-section of the Criminal Law (Amendment) Act 1935, which forbade importation, ceased to be part of the law.

This was a major historic achievement for the women of Ireland and all credit must be given to Mrs Mary McGee of Skerries, County Dublin who brought her action after a contraceptive device had been seized by the customs authorities while it was in the post. Having lost her case in the High Court she appealed to the Supreme Court and won. However, the Supreme Court ruling made little difference to the availability of contraceptives in Ireland. It simply meant that Customs and Excise officers no longer had the right to confiscate contraceptives at the point of importation. It was still illegal to sell, display or advocate the use of contraceptives in Ireland. Of course the Catholic hierarchy's attitude to contraception remained unchanged but their ability to influence legislation was in decline.

The law prohibiting the sale of contraceptives remained in force until 16 July 1974. Even the passing of the legislation was not without its comical aspects with the Taoiseach of the day Mr Liam Cosgrave voting against his own Government's Bill.

The wide availability of contraceptives coupled with education has had a great influence on the size of the Irish family in the late-1990s. Gone are the days when large families were the norm. More and more families are very conscious of limiting the number of children and giving the very best to the few children they have. During the past fifteen years or so I have noticed enormous changes in family life. One does not need statistics to prove every change. Take for example the number of women in the labour force – they are not all young, highly-educated executives. Women of all age groups have chosen to embrace a career of their choice outside their homes – there is a strong sense of independence and desire to make a life of their own. This is to be applauded and welcomed. At the same time it is pertinent to raise the question, "Has the traditional, Irish family disappeared altogether?" The answer to this would have to be "yes", in the major cities and towns of Ireland and Dublin in particular.

People I know who live in the country keep reminding me that the family is safe and sound in rural country areas. The young professional people – most of them single and from the country who live in my neighbourhood – impressed upon me that the strong fabric of family life as it existed even ten years ago is beginning to come apart at the seams even in the heart of the country. Subjects such as co-habitation, extra-marital affairs, separation, never mind divorce and homosexuality that would have been frowned upon and never openly discussed in those days are beginning to have their effect on family life even in places far away from the cities and large towns of Ireland. A group of mothers with young adult children in a country village helped me to understand some of the changes.

> Times have changed, our children do not worry too much about the rules and regulations laid down for so long by the Catholic Church anymore. They are more educated, they are not particularly worried about what the neighbours or relations will have to say, if they choose to live with their partners there is nothing we can really do any more. Of course we are worried and concerned about pre-marital sex, drugs and alcohol. We just hope they will make happy and healthy lives for themselves. They are most certainly better off than we ever were.

There is no doubt that most 'country' parents are prepared to be more flexible and are prepared to welcome their children into the family irrespective of whether they are single mothers, homosexuals or living with their partners.

Still as one young person put it, "Life is much better in the country than in Dublin, I cannot wait for the weekends to get away from here, life in Dublin is all about money, fashion, cars and houses in the 'right' areas. I could never afford to buy a small home in County Dublin. I am hoping for a transfer to a town nearer my own home. We in the country still have some sort of community life." It is understandable that life in rural areas would be different from that in cities and towns in any part of the world but there is no doubt that some of the changes taking place in Ireland seem to have happened rapidly during the past few years. This is basically the result of widely available educational opportunities both at second and third-level, better employment prospects, more disposable income, new shopping centres, shopping seven days a week, increased mobility within the nation, international travel, more opportunities to take time out and work on a temporary basis abroad and return home and, more importantly, the influence of the media and television. The membership of the EU has also had a major impact on our way of life.

Unmarried mothers

Marriage, children and family were considered to be the norm in Ireland until recently. The conception of children outside of marriage was frowned upon not only by the families of young girls but also by the community in which they lived. During the early part of 1998 a powerful television documentary on Channel 4 told us about the tragic experiences of the young women sent away to Ireland's Magdalene Asylums for their supposed sexual misconduct. Four Irish-Catholic women who were condemned as teenagers to a harrowing institutional life talked about the cruelties inflicted on them by the nuns in charge of the asylum. The film left us in no doubt about the sexual intolerance in 20th century Ireland. These women – unmarried mothers – were shunned and shut away from the 'respectable' public, and the powers that be simply turned a blind eye and deaf ear to their predicament. Their children referred to as 'illegitimate' were either adopted or remained locked away in orphanages. It was not until October 1983 that the government abolished the term 'illegitimacy' as a legal definition in this country.

Until the early 1980s the situation of women who became pregnant outside marriage especially in towns and villages outside Dublin had not really changed. Even in Dublin some families found it very difficult to cope with the shame of their unmarried daughters' pregnancies. Quite a number of these young pregnant women from Dublin and the rest of the country went to Britain, for anonymity and gave birth to their children away from the love and care of their immediate families, or to have abortions. Some women though did carry their pregnancies to term in Dublin and had their babies with the support and care of host families – thanks to the caring agencies who placed them, in the first instance with these families in Dublin.

Here we are a modern, affluent and sophisticated western nation about to move into a new millennium and still we see more and more young women from all socio-economic backgrounds, travelling to Britain for abortions. Various groups of people continue to argue vociferously about the need to ensure that abortion is never legalised in Ireland, and the problem seems to be that very little is being done about the plight of all the women who travel elsewhere for abortions. The clear message is as long as Ireland's hands are clean all is well – an Irish solution to an Irish problem.

If there is one topic that has been very hotly discussed, debated and argued during my 30 years in Ireland, I can say with confidence it is abortion. The matter is yet to be resolved to the satisfaction of everyone. Whether that is humanly possible remains to be seen. Politicians of all parties are in a dilemma on this very delicate subject. One cannot but admire those Irish people who refuse to see any grey areas in the matter of abortion, and who have over the years maintained that they are working for the common good of the Irish society.

Single Mothers

As opposed to the unmarried mothers of the 1950s-1980s, the terms 'single mother' and 'single parent' have become more widely used during the past few years. Ireland has moved from heaping shame and disgust on unmarried mothers and their families to a total acceptance of single parenthood. In the recent past there has been an unprecedented increase in the number of single mothers in Ireland. There are various schools of thought on this matter. In today's Ireland it seems, it would be unwise to talk about the 'norm' – after all, what is normality? Often in discussions relating to parents and families the point is made that simply because a father, a mother and children have composed, until recently, a 'traditional' family, it does not necessarily follow that is the only norm. As long as one caring parent, be it a mother or father, caters for the needs of their child, or children, all is well.

On the other hand there are those with the view that the traditional family is all-important. There is also a degree of unhappiness among some hard-working tax-payers that single motherhood is on the increase because of all the benefits that can be received by single mothers from the government. Surely very few young women deliberately set out to embark on pregnancy at a young age just to avail of the benefits? Could it be that women have become more independent and wish to take charge of their own lives in modern, Irish society? Could it be a reaction to the Catholic Church and its very rigid teachings over a very long period of time? Could it be that those women who feel they have not been successful in society in terms of education, profession and self-sufficiency derive a sense of fulfilment via motherhood? Could it be an escape from difficult, over-crowded homes ridden with poverty, alcoholism, physical, verbal and sexual abuse? Could it be a combination of these and other factors?

Just three years ago visiting a poor home in Dublin just before Christmas I found it extremely difficult to believe that a mother, a father and their fourteen children could possibly live in that very small dwelling – how could those children possibly be fully nourished, and be given all the attention, care and comfort they need by the parents? Yet the mother's happy smiles and laughter spoke volumes about her love for those children. She was also happy that two of her older children were single mothers and their children were living with her as well. The one lesson I learned from that visit was that people like me should not rush to impose our 'middle class' values on those who are proud of their own values and culture.

Over the past few months all the discussions I had with many people from different sectors of the community failed to deliver a single reason for the increase in the number of single mothers in Ireland. However, a psychologist and a social worker identified the following factors: alcohol, drugs, television and videos, the breakdown of family units, a decline in the influence of the Catholic Church, the absence of friendship and courtship between boys and girls, a lack of respect for each other and, above all, a lack of education about life and responsibilities at a very early stage.

At least the education is available now and one can only hope that things will improve in years to come. I talked to a few young boys and girls outside a post office where the girls, who were single mothers, were waiting to collect their allowances. They were between fifteen and seventeen years of age. The girls could see nothing wrong with being single mothers. Why didn't they take precautions before having sex? Did they not know about safe sex? The boys stepped in to give me answers. "It's up to the woman to make sure she won't get pregnant." My jaws remained wide open for a good few minutes after hearing that answer. "At what age did you become sexually active?" I asked the boys without realising that I had not phrased the question properly. One of the boys quipped, "Wha, wha do you mean?" I explained and the young man smartly dressed in designer garments said, "I was fifteen I think." I also learned that some of the boys took a part of the single mother's allowance, "That was the deal made with the girls who were entitled to their allowance," said another young boy. Just incredible!

Some women, who were listening to me talking to the young people joined the conversation. Whatever the reasons, the time has arrived to stop being politically correct but have the will to implement certain worthwhile changes to the current social welfare system in the first instance. No civilised society should deprive any citizen of their basic needs but careful consideration should be given to eradicate the culture of dependency. Nine out of ten people I interviewed maintained that the 'handouts' to single mothers was one major factor in the escalation of young women becoming single mothers.

Every effort should be made to channel as many resources as possible into primary education. There is no doubt that more and more effort and energy is being channelled into the education of today's young, compared to ten years ago, but there is more to be done. Disadvantaged children in particular need more time and attention in primary school. Children are growing much faster, both physically and mentally, they spend an inordinate amount of time in front of televisions often without much supervision or direction, they are engulfed by the 'video culture' and more and more children are surfing the internet.

Over the years politicians and educators have continually talked about full participation of every child in education. There is no doubt more and more children are being educated. I am also aware of new sex education programmes in our schools. I thought with the introduction of biology in the second-level school curriculum more of our young people would become aware of the facts of life. I was wrong of course. Perhaps with broader education, available at an earlier age, on the importance of friendship, courtship and a healthy relationship being prerequisites to human reproduction, young people of both sexes may steer away from irresponsible sexual practices to live fuller and happier lives.

Separation, Divorce and Lone Parents

In 1978, the year our only child was born, a friend of mine said, "Do you know in this country there is no escape for those people caught in a bad marriage? The Church and the State keep pretending that in Ireland marital breakdowns just do not happen." I also recall a conversation I had with a lady who was in great distress having packed her bags and left her family home. "I have had enough for 40 years, I could not stand it any more. I have just arrived in Dublin and have nowhere to go to – not yet anyway." I sat there and admired her courage and determination to make a life of her own. "Bravo," I exclaimed. "You will be OK." Indeed it was a very courageous decision in those days – an age before women felt empowered, independent and self-sufficient – to walk away from a difficult marital situation.

The Women's Liberation Movement was beginning to make some impact on the attitudes ordinary Irish women had towards men, family, religion and society. The sense of subservience to men, dependence (of married women) on their husbands and fear of being ostracised by their community and the Catholic Church began to diminish. Women were ready to break away from violent and difficult marriages and make their own lives. By the late 1980s there were enormous changes and there was no more suffering in silence – women were ready to fight for their rights.

Indeed times have changed. More and more people, men and women, were making decisions about their own lives. By the early-1980s there was an increased demand for divorce to be legalised in Ireland. Why should so many women and men caught in bad marriages remain together? Why should separated people not have the freedom to embark on new relationships and have a second chance to enter matrimony and have children? I could not believe how vociferous women had become compared to their counterparts in the 1960s and 1970s.

There were times I wondered quietly what I would do if my marriage fell apart but took consolation in the fact that as an immigrant I could pack my bags and run somewhere else. I have no family here, I have no roots but I have a daughter – so it would not be simple or easy to flee. It is so easy to fight for the common good of the country but what about real human suffering? I asked a friend of mine who refused to see the need for divorce in Ireland. She quoted all sorts of figures and facts from other countries to impress upon me the ill-effects of separation and divorce. I listened impassively but felt very strongly that the time had arrived to remove the constitutional ban on divorce in Ireland. It was 1986 and I will always remember it – despite all the progress I had witnessed since the late 1960s the referendum confirmed the Republic of Ireland's constitutional ban on divorce. So that was that!

"There is no other place like Ireland anywhere in the world

and I don't think there ever will be. Ireland is unique in many ways." I wrote to my father. He replied, "Yes, I read all about the referendum on divorce in our newspapers – strange country. It must have something to do with their religion. We have divorce here but not many avail of it – people would be too embarrassed. It just would not be acceptable or respectable to be a divorcee and don't you ever contemplate that road. It would bring so much shame to our family." I just could not see why it would be shameful to be a divorcee but refrained from furthering my point of view with him. I did hope that the attitude of the Irish people would change towards the question of divorce but was pleasantly surprised when it happened within a decade. In 1995 people voted in another divorce referendum and statutory provision was made for divorce in Ireland. I hardly hear anyone discussing the merits and demerits of separation or divorce these days. I wonder what Mr Des Hanafin is thinking – I admired his single-minded attitude to matters such as divorce and abortion and his strong Catholic faith.

Testament to the changes in attitudes, which have swept Ireland, is the fact that the Taoiseach, Bertie Ahern, is separated and living with his partner. This is in stark contrast to the wholesome family values espoused by the current leaders of both the UK and the US. Is this proof of Irish maturity and tolerance or merely our ability to turn a blind eye to that which we do not want to see?

Despite all the changes, some of which were long overdue, I believe that there seems to have been a gradual change towards what is, and is not, socially acceptable in the areas of teenage pregnancies, single mothers, separation, divorce, homosexuality and co-habitation, and I welcome the removal of social stigmas on certain issues. However, have some of us become so afraid to say certain changes in our way of life are not socially acceptable? Are we allowing a total free reign and in doing so putting the very fabric of our society in jeopardy?

I would like to think that we, as a society, are going through a transitional phase and that the time will come when we shall begin to question the merits and demerits of certain elements of social change and behaviour. Modern life has become laden with fashions that come and go. Life itself seems to have become one big fashionable item, dictated by the media. The media is our major 'guru' and we seem unwilling to question it. People in Ireland once had a similar attitude towards the Church. The difference however, is that the media provides us with a service, they feed the almost insatiable appetite the public has for information and news. In some ways it seems that we are the ones who have created the monster that is mass media. The Church is now under scrutiny from the media and it appears to me that it has gone into a permanent, pupal stage. In the final analysis, people will have to take responsibility for their lives, attitudes and behaviour, but after 30 years of living in Ireland, I, myself, am afraid to voice my fears and concerns for the gradual decline of some good, solid, 'tried and tested' family values.

> . . . the scale of marriage breakdown revealed by our census and labour survey statistics does not appear to me to be compatible with the sense of parental obligation to children which was traditionally a feature of our society, and indeed of other societies elsewhere. For a large and apparently growing minority of parents, a belief in their right to pursue what they see as their "right" to personal happiness outside the marriage union seems to have replaced the former sense of obligation to spouse and children.
>
> Dr Garret Fitzgerald
> *The Irish Times*, 15 August 1998

Chapter 5

Education: are we on the right road?

> For education has not to do with the manufacturing of things, but with the fostering and growth of things.
>
> Padraic Pearse
> *The Philosophy of Education*, November 1904

The late-1960s and early-1970s were an exciting period in the field of education in Ireland. For the first time biology as a science subject was introduced into our second-level curriculum, a brand new Bachelor of Education degree course replaced the teacher training certificate, training colleges became Colleges of Education, a new primary school curriculum was introduced and new Regional Technical Colleges were established. I was very privileged to have been associated with biological education in the academic and technical sectors. I also enjoyed writing schoolbooks for biology and travelled extensively around the country through my involvement with the winter and summer teachers' courses in biology organised by the Department of Education. I felt very welcome even in remote parts of Ireland, met not only teachers but people from other walks of life, and learned a great deal about the landscape, culture and heritage of Ireland. Incidentally, none of my employers asked me for a work permit – they were happy to utilise my intellectual abilities and I was grateful for the opportunities that came my way.

Technical education was long overdue in Ireland and the Technical Colleges were very welcome additions to the already well-established academic universities. Many Irish graduates and post-graduates with experience in academic, technical and industrial fields were recruited to the staff of the Regional Technical Colleges. However, a number of graduates and post-graduates without any teaching or industrial experience also found themselves on the staff of these colleges. The challenges which faced all the newly recruited staff were enormous. New courses had to be devised, laboratories had to be equipped but above all there was the urgent task of selling these colleges and the courses to Leaving Certificate students in second-level and vocational schools.

During those early years, the principals and staff of the Regional Technical Colleges went around second-level schools to explain the courses available and encourage the students to apply for places on them. There were no queues of prospective students and I was quick to learn that Irish students and parents did not think very highly of vocational or technical education. There was a snobbish element attached to attending a prestigious university. Yet Ireland was attracting a number of foreign industries which needed well-qualified technicians, technologists and engineers especially in the electronic, pharmaceutical, chemical, agricultural and food sectors.

Thanks to the vision of those who formulated the policies on education (and the late Donogh O'Malley in particular), the late-1960s, and early-1970s also saw the arrival of brand new National Institutes of Higher Education (NIHE), first in Limerick followed a few years later by its counterpart in Dublin: these were later to become the University of Limerick and Dublin City University. For the first time, Ireland offered varied third-level educational opportunities to young students graduating from the post-primary sector. I looked forward to helping with the development of education in the years to come.

However, the more I looked at the road education in Ireland was taking in the late-1980s and early-1990s, the more concerned I became. My fears were a reflection of those held by Ronald Dore in 1976 and in the submission made by the *Conference of Religious of Ireland* to the Minister for Education as recently as March 1998.

> . . . the more widely education certificates are used for occupational selection; the faster the rate of qualification inflation; and the more examination-oriented schooling becomes, at the expense of genuine education.
>
> Ronald Dore
> *The Diploma Disease*, 1976

> The points system for entry to third-level education is a way to help keep the poor people poor.
>
> The Leaving Certificate curriculum focuses on a narrow range of academic skills and neglects many other qualities which young people need for life and

> work; it places an unhealthy emphasis on competition and excessive individualism; it leads to young people choosing careers on the basis of exploiting their points.
>
> Conference *of Religious of Ireland's* submission to the Minister for Education
> *The Irish Times*, 6 March 1998

Ireland had always taken great pride in the broad education available to its young people attending second-level schools as opposed to the highly specialised curriculum of the GCSE ('A' Level) courses in English schools. The Leaving Certificate was considered to be a good qualification with which to enter the job market. However, the 1980s and, in particular the early-1990s, ushered in some drastic changes to the educational system: changes made essentially to meet the demands of employment.

Third-level education became necessary and extremely competitive. With the introduction of free education in the late-1960s, the number of school leavers looking for places in the universities and other third-level colleges far outstripped the number of places available. A fairer system of entry into colleges had to be put in place to deal with the large number of applications. Thus the points system arrived on the educational scene. It was, indeed, a very fair system that was based on merit. What no-one foresaw was the emphasis students and their parents would place on gaining the relevant number of points in the Leaving Certificate examination to get places in some 'prestigious' university courses at the expense of pressure-free, enjoyable learning years at the post-primary level. The ability and aptitude of students to follow their chosen courses of study in the third-level establishments became secondary to the need to gain the points required to enter the 'best' universities. The late Christina Murphy, editor of the *Education Times Supplement* and her team of journalists were also pushing reams and reams of paper full of advice on how to study for the Leaving Certificate examination, how to apply for a place in college, how to progress from a certificate to a diploma course and on to a degree course. The emphasis seemed to be on how to get a diploma or a degree.

'The Diploma-Degree Disease' had gripped the students and their parents. Having read a book entitled *The Diploma Disease* by Ronald Dore published in 1976, I began to worry about the very foundations upon which the educational system in Ireland is based. Are we taking a short-term view of education? Dore stated clearly: " . . . learning, knowing, understanding, thinking, 'civilise'; that education, the cultivation of human minds and spirits, is the foundation of a good and economically productive society; that the improvement of education is a means to a better society." Schooling in Ireland as in some other nations around the world in the words of Dore has become "ritualistic, tedious, suffused with anxiety and boredom, destructive of curiosity and imagination; in short, anti-educational". Yet, the Irish students have no alternative – the all-important business of earning a qualification is equated with gainful employment.

Even with the points in their school bags, not all the students manage to find a place in the course of study they want or in the college of their choice. It is a lottery system. And so, the points-gathering process of school education is still in place, for want of a better method of assessing our children who wish to proceed to third-level institutions.

If education in Ireland is about getting into a college and following a course of study which will enable our young people to seek, find and slot into a job then we are taking a very short-term view of education. During the past fifteen years or so the various ministers of education and the industries, have been obsessed with 'education for industry'. More and more emphasis has been placed on tailoring third-level courses to suit the demands of an ever growing and expanding industrial sector. Out went the principles of good general education. On the one hand there is so much talk about our confident, young, vibrant, educated workforce while on the other, there appears to be a general and gradual decline in the ability of the same young graduates to write well, spell correctly, or employ a wide vocabulary in their speech. I have no doubt they are good at doing a specific job they are employed to do, but how will they interact to create the type of society we all want to see.

What about education for life? What about the development of the whole person? Education should be about thinking, enquiring, researching, analysing, understanding, explaining, communicating and above all continuing to add to and apply this knowledge to the needs and demands of a job and life, particularly in the fast-changing modern world. Generally well informed, educated people should have no trouble adapting to the specifics of an employment situation. Unfortunately, education today seems to be not about education in the real sense. Education has become a major industry – a production line without quality assurance.

For example, think of the middle-class parents of the 1980s and 1990s. As a member of the parents' council of a school in the early-1990s I sat and listened for hours when these parents argued about one subject – Honours Maths. Why should a schoolboy or a girl be put under pressure by parents who for one reason or other believe that certain subjects are more prestigious than others? The same applies when it comes to choosing a course at university: medicine, law, veterinary science, pharmacy and accountancy are definitely top of the list. Robotic learning under pressure to get the highest number of points – a situation created by the heavy demand for certain courses – is all that is needed to become, for example, a doctor. Never mind the aptitude, suitability and other personal criteria essential to be a doctor or a teacher or a vet!

Training of our students to be teachers at primary and second-level is one area that should receive maximum and regular attention from the Department of Education. Primary school education in particular, is the most important foundation stone in a child's life. In an ideal world teachers should be handpicked for this sector as sound knowledge alone is never enough to be a good teacher. Communicating that knowledge and encouraging every child to learn according to that child's ability is absolutely vital. Not all of us – however intelligent or clever – are good communicators. A vital prerequisite to be a teacher is the ability to communicate effectively and it is very important for the right calibre of students to be selected by Colleges for Education. Not all students with the required number of points will turn out to be excellent teachers. When the Bachelor of Education degree programme was introduced in the 1970s, I believed that the whole approach to teacher training would change. Has it?

The one question that must be addressed in addition to the review proposed recently by the current Minister for Education Micheal Martin, is, "How well equipped are the lecturers who train our young teachers in both primary and second-level? Should they be encouraged and required to spend a certain amount of time teaching in primary and second-level schools and have the experience of classrooms before embarking on full-time lecturing?" Surely the surgeon who trains the medical students would be expected to have first-hand experience of surgical procedures before he or she takes on the training of future surgeons. Shouldn't the same apply to the staff in Colleges and Schools of Education in the universities if they have to train the future teachers? A string of degrees in education or other subjects without actual practical knowledge and experience of primary school teaching just cannot and will not confer upon the lecturers the necessary skills to train young student teachers. Equally, bright students, with all the 'A's in the world will not necessarily make good teachers at any level. The one profession, which needs the very best communicators, in my opinion, is teaching at first and second-level and I wonder how our teachers are selected to teach in both sectors. Teacher assessment is as important as student assessment. The very best teachers should also be remunerated accordingly.

It is encouraging to see some very able students with good Leaving Certificate results choose to follow the courses of their choice in faculties other than medicine or law or the other so-called 'prestigious' disciplines. Some of my own acquaintances tend to dismiss my daughter because she is not going to be a doctor, lawyer or whatever. I am always amused by the expression on their faces when told that "no, she is not following a course in medicine". Parents being interested in the welfare and education of their offspring is normal, natural and desirable, but, being obsessed with pushing their children to perform in areas not suited to their natural ability is detrimental to the very health and happiness of their children. I am afraid quite a number of our young students are under pressure to perform well at school and college because of parental expectations and because of the current points-oriented examination and selection system.

Another undesirable element that has become prevalent in the educational system of Ireland since the 1980s, is the mushrooming of grind schools. There is nothing wrong with some children getting some help with certain subjects from a teacher or a tutor after normal school hours. Grind schools are flourishing because parents and their children want them, and because parents are prepared to pay for them. They see these private establishments as their offspring's major hope of gathering the essential points in the Leaving Certificate examination. Grind schools themselves are a major money-making industry in modern Ireland. Are our regular schools and teachers not able to cope with providing adequate knowledge to the students to ensure that they perform well in their examinations? Why don't the parents and students trust the teachers to do their job well? Ireland has a lot of very hard-working and committed teachers, a fact that should be recognised.

Recently a principal explained to me, "There is nothing wrong with our teachers. We have some excellent teachers and there are some that are not very good. The point is, the grind schools manage to hunt and recruit some of our best teachers – such teachers feel flattered and very privileged to teach in these schools. However, there are a number of students who do not attend these grind schools and many still manage to achieve very good results." On a matter of principle as a former teacher, I did not see the need to send my daughter to a grind school. Nor did she ask to attend one. She attended a good school, which had excellent teaching staff, who also ensured the development of the 'person' in all their students.

Why do parents think that a grind school is necessary to get results? The same principal explained, "One parent talks about the results achieved by his or her child as a direct result of attending grind schools, and the next parent feels guilty and finds the money to send the child to a grind school. And so the grind schools keep flourishing. Furthermore, some parents really believe free education cannot be all that good." The most disappointing development in the 1990s is that a number of students from regular second-level schools in Dublin and other cities are leaving at the end of the transition year to enrol as full-time students in some popular grind schools. I believe that a well-structured second-level school education is very desirable for the development of a young person. Cramming facts and figures to the exclusion of everything else, is not a healthy passport to their future life in an increasingly demanding and competitive world.

All through my life in Ireland, politicians and other leaders in the community never failed to talk about the educational opportunities for the disadvantaged in our society. Dr Daniel O'Hare, President of Dublin City University recently called for equal access to third-level education by 2010 and said the access schemes in place at most universities, to encourage student entry from disadvantaged backgrounds, had been 'minimal' in their effect (*The Irish Times*, 10 March 1998). Why is Ireland reluctant to examine this question of non-participation by the disadvantaged in the whole educational system, instead making politically correct statements? A man, who happens to be a window cleaner, explained to me, "People in Ireland do not understand our culture. We have a different way of looking at things. We just won't fit into your culture because we are happy where we are. Why will we throw away what the government gives us? And, don't take me wrong. We are entitled to all those benefits." Therein lies the problem.

Contrast this with someone from a nation that is poor and who would not receive a penny from the government, because there is not the money for the government to hand out. A truly sorry state of affairs when there must be so many people who genuinely need some help from the government. I am not discussing the merits and demerits of the social welfare system as it operates here or elsewhere. From my experience of some poor nations, where there is free primary and post-primary education many poor people look upon education as the only way out of poverty. This is even the case in countries where there is no free education.

I have seen poor parents in Nigeria arriving with a handful of dirty notes, often smelling of fish, straight from their fish stalls in the market, to pay their children's school and boarding fees. I have seen people from lower castes in my own native Ceylon embracing education and making full use of the free education to make their way out of extreme poverty – real poverty – and hope to become gainfully employed and lead better lives. Take the Harijans of India whom Mahatma Gandhi affectionately called "children of God". I was heartened to see them part of the mainstream society in India as recently as January 1998, thanks to various positive discriminatory measures put into place in schools and colleges by the government of India. They have, of course, a long way to go before they are fully integrated into Indian society.

Has the time arrived to examine our 'hand-out' system and put in place a more suitable one to meet the demands of a modern, prosperous 'new' Ireland? Indeed it has, and let us stop producing more and more green, white and blue papers on every issue that comes our way. Let us for a change look at the real problem. The politicians alone cannot and will not change the system. To be elected means saying the right words and doing the right thing by the voters. Fair enough, we need politicians in a democratic nation, but more importantly we need those with vision, commitment, dedication and courage to be able to bring about worthwhile changes in the existing social welfare system. Education for everyone can only come about when everyone avails of it because they want to, irrespective of their background.

Simply talking about the disadvantaged or providing equal opportunities is not enough. Why, with free education available in Ireland since the late-1960s, are more and more people from disadvantaged backgrounds not moving on to third-level education? Now that we have free education in universities and other third-level colleges, money is not the sole factor restricting participation by all sectors of the community. Should we consider putting in place some worthwhile positive discriminatory measures to encourage the young people from disadvantaged backgrounds to avail of education? I fully endorse the point Dr O'Hare made, "we [must] radically change our view of the place of mature students in our universities . . . they must be a major facilitator in solving the problem of access by the disadvantaged" (*The Irish Times*, 10 March 1998).

However, if as Dr O'Hare says, "the future Ireland, if it is to grow in prosperity, will need all its population to be educated to the limits of their ability" then what sort of education should the nation provide for everybody? Surely it should not be the type of education our young people are receiving today. As an outsider looking in, I have watched with dismay the decline in standards of general education. It is not the fault of the students if they do not have time to think outside the demanding points-gathering examination system that is in operation.

An experienced educator in science giving a paper at the Royal Dublin Society early in 1998 said, "There are some students with 'A's and 'B's in Biology arriving in our universities – ill-equipped to handle a microscope, they do not know which end of the microscope to look through." I could not believe that after nearly 30 years of free education and emphasis on teaching science in all our schools such a statement could have been made about our education system. Some Leaving Certificate students I interviewed explained to me that they had been advised by their teachers to leave out sections of the course in some subjects and concentrate on those from which examination questions are generated. Of course it is not the fault of the teachers or the students. The teachers and students are under constant pressure to work towards a Leaving Certificate examination that decides the future of our young people.

There does not seem to be enough time to enjoy and learn science subjects from laboratory work. There are no Leaving Certificate examinations on the practical content of science subjects. Furthermore, teachers who teach science and other practical subjects in second-level schools have no help from qualified laboratory technicians to set up practical work. Is it not time each second-level school was allowed a qualified, full-time science technician? The whole emphasis seems to be on learning facts or ready-made answers to questions – thanks to the grind schools they are available in plenty, which can then be regurgitated on answer papers in examination halls. One principal explained to me, "I have mothers arriving in my school asking me to suggest to my teachers that ready-made answers to questions be given to their children taking the Leaving Certificate examination." The whole system of second-level education is driven by the needs of our middle class students and their parents to get into that tertiary sector and preferably well-established universities.

A few years ago at a conference on education in Britain, a member of the panel made this remark to me privately, " All of us are not 5 star people, our education should cater for the 1,2,3,4 and 5 star pupils from all socio-economic backgrounds." Are we putting all our students under pressure to perform all the way? Today most students emerging from our second-level schools are expected to, or want to, attend post Leaving Certificate colleges, third-level technical colleges or universities and emerge with a certificate, diploma or degree and embark upon a job! Is this the be-all and end-all of our very modern educational system? What about the personal development of the student?

Through our 'education industry' quite a number of our young people seem to be emerging without the basics. It is unbelievable that despite all the educational facilities available for the past 30 years, Ireland "stands out as a country with one of the greatest literacy problems among 16 to 25-year olds" according to a recent OECD literary survey of eleven countries. This survey also showed that 25 per cent of Irish people were at the lowest level of literacy, a figure which is 50 per cent higher than in other advanced countries surveyed. There is also evidence in this survey of basic reading problems among the school-going population. Among 14-year olds, three times as many boys as girls have worrying literacy problems. Surely this must cause concern among all our educators and parents. Not for a moment would I suggest that educating the young today in is an easy task. The stresses and strains of teaching are colossal. Lack of discipline, lack of respect for teachers, teacher harassment and, at times, even violence in the classroom, do not make for a congenial atmosphere for imparting knowledge.

Perhaps the time has arrived to examine the alternatives to entry to our third-level educational institutions and remove some of the pressures placed on the students and their teachers. It is encouraging that the Points Commission under the chairmanship of Professor Aine Hyland is examining the whole issue. There are other areas which are in need of reappraisal too. Is it necessary to walk straight out of a second-level school into a university, teacher training college or technical college? Why should the students not complete a transition year after the Leaving Certificate examination? Why not allow students to take a break from formal education for a year or more and enter a temporary career at an earlier age, learning on the job and proceeding to further education as mature students? For example students who wish to be trained as teachers could begin as pupil-teachers, future engineers could commence work as craftsmen and so on. If this sounds far-fetched at least it has one major advantage – students who wish to enter tertiary education will at least be mature.

Alternatively a year spent on the campuses of our universities, technical and teacher training colleges studying a core curriculum compulsory for all students with freedom to choose any two or three subjects of their choice and enjoy reading, learning, researching, discussing, writing and then being selected to proceed with formal certifiable courses – degrees, diplomas or certificates – would be far more preferable to the education entry system that is available today.

During the early-1970s I thought the establishment of the Regional Technical Colleges was a step in the right direction. Today, after nearly 25 years these colleges, students, staff and the Ministers for Education seem to be more concerned about the names of these colleges – Institutes of Technology – than about the level of education they are providing. Are we to understand that there still exists a second-class attitude to these colleges by the parents and students, and therefore, a change of name may put them on an equal footing with the long established universities and other colleges? At least my discussion on this topic with those associated with these establishments clearly demonstrated that it is really a hangover from the days of the vocational education and vocational schools, which catered for the lower socio-economic groups in Ireland.

I remember the vocational schools being referred to as 'Techs'. There was a snobbish attitude too amongst upper and middle class people towards vocational education. A sample of students I spoke to do not feel totally happy about being in these Institutes of Technology. "Our preference would be to attend a university, unfortunately we did not get the points to make it to the university. We hope to get our diplomas and transfer to universities later on," one student said. There is a perceived notion that universities are better than the Technical Colleges (or Institutes of Technology as they are now called), amongst parents and students. Perhaps an education-break mentioned earlier and placing every student graduating from the schools by a process of selection in various temporary careers, right across the spectrum of employment, may just help to root out the obsession with our universities.

The task may be enormous but the need is immediate. Politicians and educators would be very short-sighted if they sit back and continue to claim that Ireland has the best system of education and the best educated young people in the world. The time has come to consider the importance of an overall, general education and consider the personal development of students. No-one could possibly argue against education for jobs, or specific training for the skills required to work in specific industries, but not to the exclusion or at the expense of an education that will also equip our young people to step into their future as well-rounded and well-adjusted people.

I hope that our young graduates coming out of the universities and other third-level colleges won't be like the infamous Generation X those (who came-of-age in the 1980s) of our neighbouring country. Dr Jane Sturges, a research fellow at Birbeck College in London having analysed the responses by 200 graduates to questionnaires revealed that universities are not merely turning out students who are deficient in literacy and numeracy, but are also producing a guileless generation with a set of assumptions that could amount to an attitude problem for employers!

> It is hard to believe, listening to the almost cosy consensus about the Republic's wonderful education system, that international studies have found something quite different. A succession of reports by the Organisation for Economic Co-operation and Development (OECD) have revealed that the Republic had the highest ratio of pupils to teachers in Europe for primary schools. Irish teachers are among the best paid in Europe but work shorter hours. The government spends less per primary pupil then its counterparts, and primary schools are paupers in comparison with secondaries and well-financed universities.
>
> John Burns,
> *The Sunday Times*, 26 July 1998

Appendix 1

Higher Education: developing people or feeding the economy?

Aoife Toomey

(This was a prize-winning entry in the *Soapbox* competition organised by the Chartered Institute of Management Accountants, April 1998)

The portals of the world are flung open, the opportunities and experiences are limitless, the world is your oyster and the future looks bright. These are some of the thoughts that flew around my already full head upon entering third-level education. Student days are the best of your life: never again will it be this good, the carefree days with limited responsibility and limitless opportunity. The prospects for each undergraduate are placed firmly in his or her own hands, but with all that a third-level educational establishment is purported to offer you, they seem as bright as possible.

Yet often the experience falls somewhat short of the expectation. There are, of course, many wonderful opportunities placed at our convenience, but the atmosphere is somewhat anonymous and uncaring. University was, as far as I knew, supposed to nurture and develop all the latent potential that had only been hinted at during second-level education, not only in academic terms, but in personal ones too. Having finally reached that threshold between childhood and maturity, this is our chance to become the best that we can be: to give back to society that which those of us who have reached this level of education are lucky enough to have, and to further develop and ensure progress for those who are still to come. The torch has been passed on by those who have gone before, there should be a sense of our responsibility to become the best we can, in life not just in the labour market, yet this too is somehow lacking.

As under-graduates, third-level education seems to be part of the rat race, not a golden opportunity, not a chance to explore and discover, not even a hallowed place of learning where knowledge is loved for its own sake. Rather it is an institution that feeds the already crowded treadmill of over-worked and under-paid, white-collar workers. Of course some of those undergraduates reach unparalleled levels of success, there is undoubtedly an impressive list of CEOs and MDs that have passed through the gates of Trinity College or UCD, or any one of our higher educational institutions, but there are also those who are entirely self-made, having never progressed far in the formal education stakes. Sadly, attending university seems to have ceased to be an end in itself, a way to expand knowledge and learning, and has instead become a means to an end.

Erasmus and his cronies must be rolling in their graves at how such prestigious institutions as Cambridge and Oxford or the universities of Paris and Bologna have changed. The original idea of a college was that a group of students would gather together to share academic and residential facilities and in doing so, would benefit from mutual knowledge and learning. The heated discussions and debates that ensued no doubt inspired some of the most famous theories and philosophies that are still in existence today. Now, however, competition and rivalry have replaced the original camaraderie and the job hunt has replaced the original knowledge quest. Useful knowledge is only that which pertains to an exam paper, the joy of intellect lost in the shadow of earning power.

The government's education policies have not really done much to reverse the situation, nor have the employer's attitudes. We live in a society infected with the diploma disease, where every job needs an official third-level qualification and every third-level institution needs to be a university. Gone are the days of the gradation of higher level institutions. Polytechnics in the UK and Regional Technical Colleges in Ireland have shed, rather shamefacedly, their mantle of technical and vocational training. The numbers being pushed through the system are growing at a frightening rate, with establishments almost unable to match the demand for third-level places, a pressure not relieved by the abolition of fees.

The abolition of fees was hailed as the removal of a major obstacle to equal opportunities, and yet how large, in reality, is the proportion of dis-advantaged among today's undergraduates? The reasons for such changes seem unclear, perhaps even to those that wrought them, shrouded in excellent, but indecipherable, rhetoric. Are the pressures internal or external? Are the influences economically or academically orientated? Do government decisions stem from concern for students or concern for the economy and their own political stability? Cynical it may be, but the economy seems to take priority over the student.

University, higher education, third-level – whatever label you choose to give it – this is, for the majority of us, the last phase of formal education. That is not to say we stop learning upon completion of this phase, but never again shall the opportunity to be completely immersed in learning, understanding and the realisation of your potential, present itself like this. Going to college should be about so much more than becoming qualified for a job. It should be about social skills and aptitudes, daring to be different, discovering what makes you tick, trying all the new experiences on offer, be they of a sporting, social or academic nature. Higher education should ensure that if you have used the opportunity to the best of all your abilities, you come out of those gates an able, well-rounded, capable individual with some sort of life plan that is not solely about making money. It should give each student an appetite for all aspects of life, and ensure that every one of them knows their limits, their abilities and how hard they can push themselves towards any type of goal.

Instead it appears that many of the establishments cater for the job market rather than the life market. There can be no doubt that hundreds of excellently qualified employees leave higher education every year. They will be true assets to any firm wishing to employ them, at least in terms of qualifications. Indeed with the economy booming, the future has never looked so bright for many graduates – but what of the people, as distinct from the degree holders? Other than the piece of paper clutched proudly in their hands, what else did they gain from going to college? They learned a new language, or how to operate in the business world, or how to discover new scientific wonders, but what did they learn of themselves? Did they discover a new sport, or a cause to consume their passion? Did they gain insightful knowledge that is totally unrelated to their course, but is really interesting nonetheless? Did they even learn to think for themselves, or were they too busy faithfully learning that which their textbooks deemed useful?

Some of the best tutorials I have attended were the ones that led onto not unrelated, but not completely pertinent-to-the-exam, topics. It was lateral thinking in action, discourse and disagreement over topics that interested us and that we could, however tenuously, link to our course. It was about seeing the bigger picture, the world that lies outside our minute slice of academia.

In recent years there has been a move towards fostering interdisciplinary courses, to break away from the stale trend of over-specialisation and boxed-in thinking. This is a huge step towards nurturing people instead of just creating good employees for the benefit of the economy. Surely that is the point, the crux and heart of the matter: higher education should both develop people and feed the economy.

In the end, a completely rounded person who has proved that he or she can learn and adapt is more of an asset to an employer than anything else. Someone who can think up new ideas and have original thoughts is more desirable in a work situation than someone who knows all there is to know about one topic, but knows nothing of anything else.

In the real world it is the socially skilled who shine at interviews and who are more likely to get ahead than the geniuses. Fully rounded, personable graduates who have also done well academically should be the goal of every third-level establishment. They should view themselves less as a factory that can churn out able employees, and more as a nurturer of young, gifted people who upon realising all their potential will be true assets to the whole of society. The economy is only a part of that society, how major a part is a subjective opinion to which everyone is entitled, but society will suffer if it continues to play second fiddle to the economy in the education stakes. Perhaps the saddest part is that the people to suffer most will be the students themselves, for they will be wasting the opportunity of a lifetime, to become the best they can be, in all aspects of life.

Chapter 6

On the Question of Irish Attitudes

During my early years in Dublin, people were most anxious to explain to me that there were no major 'class divisions' in Ireland. "Oh no, we do not have a class system, not like England." A product of a very rigid caste system in Ceylon, I was able to gauge who was who in Ireland. Instinctively I knew the person from the country – often described by the Dubliners as a 'culchie'. I was also able to identify the different socio-economic groups simply by listening to the way they spoke. Even the way they wore their clothes was a direct indication of their social class. I was puzzled by the constant and casual swearing by some people on the buses, at the bus stops and even in regular conversation.

I remember discussing this point with my former professor in Trinity College and he simply said, "Well brought up ladies and gentlemen would not use such words and it certainly is not a word that any lady should ever use." However much the Irish folk I met protested that there was no class system in this country, I knew there was. Groups of people I would have quietly placed in the category of middle or upper class were very conscious of the fact that they were different, and felt somewhat superior to those who did not belong to their group. I saw nothing strange in this attitude because I was so familiar with it as it operated in some Asian countries. I was also aware that the group of people identified as 'Anglo-Irish' kept their distance from the rest of the Irish people. Therefore, despite the fact the Irish people from all walks of life tried to impress upon me that there was no class system, I was not convinced.

The attitudes of the different groups of people towards each other made me wonder about this predominantly Catholic nation. Recently, an English friend who has lived here for more than 40 years told me, " I know someone who refused to collect the monthly children's allowance because she felt it was for very 'ordinary' poor people and would be embarrassed to collect it." How I wish that same lady collected her children's allowance and donated it to a charity of her choice. Such people may be few and far between but there was no doubt the Irish were very conscious of their addresses and of the social levels in their communities.

However, on the whole Irish people gave me the impression that they were aware of the needs of other people who were not as well off as themselves both within Ireland and also in other poor countries in Asia, Africa and South America. Often I would see a nun from the Little Sisters of the Poor standing at the top of Clarendon Street, even on cold winter days, collecting for the poor. I had heard about people being asked to contribute 'a penny for the black babies'. Most probably it was before I arrived in Ireland. Annual sales were held by various concerned groups of people particularly the religious orders to raise much-needed funds for the foreign missions. Coffee mornings and cake sales in private houses to raise money for the poor of the developing world were quite common too in the Ireland of the 1970s and 1980s.

Annual church collections, appeals on the radio and television by celebrities and advertisements in the national newspapers urging people to donate generously towards the needy were made by various charitable organisations especially during the pre-Easter or pre-Christmas periods which were, and are, very much part of this nation's way of life. Young students from schools and colleges took great pride in being able to organise their own ways and means of raising funds for the starving populations in distant, developing countries. I was touched by the sharing attitude of the Irish. Time and again I came to the conclusion that irrespective of the socio-economic groups to which people belonged, they were always anxious to help those who were in need. The tireless work by the Society of Vincent de Paul to help those in need cannot be matched by any other organisation in the world. As recently as February 1998, our local church appealed to its congregation to take home polythene bags distributed by members of the Society of Vincent de Paul and fill them with clean wearable clothes to be given to those in need. "What does this say about the Celtic Tiger?" I exclaimed. In the economically vibrant Ireland of 1998, boasting its millionaires and with 44,000 Irish emigrants returning to reap the comforts and benefits of a prosperous nation, there are still people looking for used clothes. However, I was heartened to see bags and bags of clothes arrive at the church the following Sunday.

Nevertheless, I found the attitude of the Irish from the big cities and towns towards those in the travelling community inexplicable. "Not in our back yards or neighbourhood, but elsewhere please" was the reply when the question of accommodating the travelling community arose. I was aghast at the vociferous opposition by a number of people in my own area when a meeting was called at the beginning of this decade to discuss the possibility of allocating a halting site with running water and sanitary facilities for the travelling people. The arguments against such a halting site at that meeting left me somewhat shaken and also worried about my own sense of belonging in this country in which I had lived and to which I had contributed for so long.

Some Irish people, who had travelled extensively or worked abroad, have told me about the parochial and to a large extent insular attitude of the nation in general. I became aware of the latent fear people had of outsiders – even those from another county in Ireland. 'Runner-in' was a term often used by country people to describe another Irish person from a different county in their very own community. My Irish husband from County Dublin was described this way in another county where we lived for a while. If people labelled a native Irishman as a 'runner-in' then how would they label me? Well and truly a foreigner, and visibly so. I have no doubt I was and am labelled in that way.

On the other hand, I hasten to make the point that even if the people in the communities in which I have lived felt that I was not one of them, they never made me feel unwelcome. On the contrary over the 30 years of my life here, I know I felt a definite sense of belonging and a sense of identity, which gave me enormous confidence to contribute positively to this country.

Yet, I could not help observing that around the early to mid-1990s a change occurred in the 'attitudes' of people to life, towards each other, to the Church and religion, indeed to almost everything in Irish society. I tried very hard to analyse the situation and why the word 'attitudes' was often used by a number of people with whom I came into contact. The 'in' words a decade ago were recession, national debt, unemployment, high inflation, rising interest rates, emigration and high income tax. On 31 December 1987, the country's national debt stood at £26,345 million! The 'yuppie' mania of Margaret Thatcher's Britain of the 1980s had not really reached the shores of Ireland, although the media did talk to some extent about 'yuppies', Dublin 4, Killiney, Foxrock and the 'chattering classes'.

In some parts of Dublin, people make comments about those who live in Dublin 4 or Foxrock. I have come into contact with a great number of people from Foxrock, Killiney and other 'fashionable' suburbs of Dublin and they do not seem to be any different from the rest of the Irish people I know. Although most are wealthier, own comfortable large homes with all the modern conveniences, large sweeping landscaped gardens, and have big, fashionable cars. Modern Ireland has become very affluent – at least some sections of the community have benefited and continue to benefit from the frequently mentioned 'Celtic Tiger'. Unlike the bygone days of the 1950s or 1960s people do not need family connections or inherited wealth to buy properties in areas which were owned by an exclusive few. All that one needs is money and more money, and that seems to be available in plenty in the Ireland of 1998. The prices of some property in Killiney, Dalkey, Foxrock and Dublin 4 seem to give a good indication of the wealth in some private hands.

On a recent visit to Cork, I noticed that it was not very different from Dublin – there were large pockets of desirable residential areas with 'fashionable', well-heeled, people. In the early-1970s when I spent some time in the city and county of Cork there was a marked difference between it and Dublin. Not any more, and as one Church of Ireland clergyman based in the heart of Cork pointed out to me "we have a Dublin 4 in Cork too". What is it? Why do we label some suburbs and their occupants be they in Dublin, Cork or Galway? Are the people living in these areas conscious of their 'superiority', simply because they are there, or are those outside so insecure or even envious that they find the need to talk about those 'superior' people? Reading some of the newspapers in Ireland I cannot help thinking that media people tend to create the divide too. Why? In Ireland, as elsewhere, useful and valuable print space is given over to trivial matters – does it matter who wore what and who attended what function or who drank and ate what?

On the one hand there are the very concerned Irish people talking, writing and reminding us of what should be done for the disadvantaged, the poor, the homeless and the illiterate, and on the other, so much energy, effort and words are channelled into utter nonsense about 'high society'. This is Ireland that had taken so much pride in being a land of the saints and scholars, land of the ordinary God-fearing and good-living people. Surely there is no need for this sea change of attitude towards money and materialism, which seems now to govern every facet of Irish life.

Some Irish people from different walks of life and age groups with whom I discussed this business of new money and materialism put forward various theories, but how about this one for sheer good-humoured unadulterated explanation, "Ah! sure we never had it before, now that we have it we might as well go to town on it – at least before we all go bust. You know we will

– all this nonsense about this 'Celtic Tiger', I have not seen it."

One of the fascinating features of the people I got to know over the years, be they from the city, county, town or country, rich or poor, was their sense of humour. Even when Irish people describe themselves as "a nation of begrudgers" I can only see the humorous side to it. Surely they do not mean a word of it. I remember praising, to one of his customers, a man who managed to build his own spacious grocer's shop having started from selling vegetables in a temporary shed at the side of the road. The sharp and quick response of the customer was, "I knew him long before he even had his shed. He used to deliver potatoes door-to-door, his father did the same too."

A good friend of mine explained to me afterwards, "We can never let someone forget their past especially if it was a humble one." Is that an Irish trait, I wonder? I could only see the funny side of the customer's words about my potato-man turned rich grocer. There does seem to be an innate inability of some to spontaneously rejoice and celebrate another person's success, and there are those who cannot refrain from making remarks such as "so, you have come up in the world". I see it as human failing and not necessarily an Irish trait. My only sadness is that some people these days, at least in Dublin, just do not seem to have the time to indulge in harmless humorous conversations. They are all busy, they are all rushing, they look tired, and they seem to be under pressure – women, men and the young as well. What a shame they just do not seem to have the time or even the energy to smile. The Irish are noted for their smiles and laughter, humour and wit, chattiness and gregarious attitude. It would be a pity if these splendid qualities were lost from the Irish nature.

If I give the impression that Dublin is Ireland, it is essentially because most of my life during the past 30 years has been lived in Dublin, and that is how it has appeared to me. On the other hand it would be right to say from my observations "there is Ireland and there is Dublin, and even in Dublin, there is Dublin and there is Dún Laoghaire". The attitudes held by people outside Dublin to certain matters concerning the society or the nation as a whole are different from those held by the Dubliners. This was very evident in the manner in which people living in different parts of the country cast their votes on major issues such as the 'Pro-Life' and 'Divorce' Referenda. The population of Dún Laoghaire, I believe, adopts a more liberal attitude to certain matters, a fact often reflected in its voting patterns. More and more of the Irish people especially those living in Dublin and major cities, through education, travel and of course the most powerful medium of television have moved away from the very conservative, Catholic Church-oriented ideas and values to embrace more liberal and society-oriented ones. Yet that is not true of many others in the rest of the nation. Take the recent referendum on divorce – the referendum was carried by the skin of its teeth!

During the summer of 1975, I was invited by a few of my new neighbours to a coffee morning. They were all young married women and almost all of them were full-time housewives. Much to my surprise, the general discussion over coffee was about men and sex. I was taken aback when one lady explained, "I would not even get undressed in our bedroom, I always do that in the bathroom." But why? What was there to be ashamed of? "We are not supposed to take pleasure in our own bodies or sexual activities, that would be sinful," the same lady continued. "Who said so?" I asked, and she reported, "the Church of course and the nuns who taught me made sure to drum that into my head – are you not a Catholic?"

This is why matters pertaining to any aspect of sex were seldom discussed openly in Ireland. It is as if sex simply did not exist here. Yet Irish families were very large. Not wishing to pry into the reasons for such an attitude to sex in normal human lives I had concluded that it must have something to do with all those Victorian values and modesty. I was wrong of course because the Catholic Church and its teachings on procreation influenced the way in which Irish Catholics looked upon sexual matters. The distinct message was that sex was not for human pleasure and those who dared to think that way were committing a sin.

In my own culture, we did not discuss sexual matters openly or freely either, but unlike here, sex and sin were not synonymous. Even my school friends who were Catholics, did not indicate to me that their Church had brainwashed them about sex, which was considered to be a very normal, human, biological need. This is why I found the attitude of the Irish to sex somewhat bizarre – surely no Church can possibly have such an influence on its flock? Why were the Irish women and men so obedient to their Church? Why were they so timid when it should be healthy to discuss matters pertaining to their religion? Somehow, it appeared to me that they had no freedom to enjoy their normal lives – at least what I considered to be normal, biological and very human!

Recently, during a conversation I had with a retired senior clergyman about the 'new' Ireland he said, "Religion dominated everything Irish for a long time, and now it is all about sex and sex scandals of the Church and society – a pity really, we also seem to be obsessed with getting more and more of the European money." To understand why a Catholic Church-dominated, ultra conservative, and in some ways a very closed, Irish society of the late-1960s and early-1970s has metamorphosed into a somewhat liberal and open one in the 1990s, it would be helpful to look back at some of the extraordinary events that have taken place during the past two decades.

1970 The Catholic hierarchy announces removal of restrictions on Catholics attending Trinity College, Dublin.

1972 A referendum in the Republic deletes from the constitution reference to the special position of the Catholic Church.

1972 A referendum in the Republic on entry to European Economic Community: for 1,041,890, against 211,981.

1972 Dermot Ryan becomes the first RC Archbishop to attend a service in Dublin's Christ Church Cathedral (Church of Ireland) since the Reformation.

1973 The Republic of Ireland becomes a member of the EEC along with the UK and Denmark.

1973 The publication of the Report of the Republic of Ireland Commission on Status of Women recommending an end to sex discrimination in employment, equal pay, maternity leave, day-care for children, marriage counselling and family planning advice.

1973 An Act abolishes the bar against continued employment of women civil servants who marry while in the service.

1973 Ireland's first woman ambassador Mary Catherine Timoney is appointed as ambassador to Sweden and Finland.

1973 In a majority decision the Supreme Court of the Republic of Ireland rules that it is unconstitutional to prohibit the importation of contraceptives. (Judgment in case taken by Mrs Mary Mc Gee against the State).

1980 Dubliner Mella Carroll becomes the first female High Court Judge in the Republic of Ireland.

1983 A 'Pro-Life' amendment to the constitution carried by 841,233 votes to 416,136.

1983 The Government abolishes the term 'illegitimacy' as a legal definition in the Republic.

1989 Judicial separation and family law reform legislation amend grounds for separation and facilitates reconciliation between estranged spouses.

1989 A Government Act prohibits incitement to hatred on account of race, religion, nationality or sexual orientation.

1990 Mary Robinson is elected President.

1991 A Government Act recognises adoptions outside the State.

1995 A Government Act regulates information services outside the State for the termination of pregnancies.

1996 The Government amends the Family Law Act to make divorce legally available in Ireland.

Looking at some of the events which have taken place especially with reference to legislation and regarding women in Irish society, it is apparent that Ireland was lagging way behind other European nations and America even though it had become a member of the European Community in 1973. In a way Ireland was only just catching up with the other countries in the Western world.

However, during my 30 years of living in Dublin, I believe one of the major players in the much needed process of change in Ireland has been the media. The power of the television was phenomenal. Those viewers who were able to tune into BBC were treated to a world not largely familiar to the Irish nation. Young and vibrant journalists and columnists of broadsheet newspapers read by the middle classes began to influence public opinion. During the last ten years in particular investigative journalism started to expose scandals within the Catholic Church. Who would have thought Bishop Eamon Casey's 'other' life involving sex and Church funds would reach the living rooms of the ordinary citizens? Who would have thought Sisters of Mercy, Christian Brothers and priests who were held in high esteem and regard by many Irish Catholic people over many decades would fall from grace almost overnight? Though I was aware of the changes (some long overdue) that were taking place gradually since my arrival, the speed with which some of the changes took place, particularly the attitudes of people to the long held traditional views about society, politics and politicians, Church and religion, family, work, money, marriage, sex and children was simply breath-taking.

I have already written of my first impressions of the Catholic Church in Ireland and Dublin in particular, and as I got to know Dublin and the rest of the country more one thing was certain – the Catholic Church had enormous power and influence in this nation. What really baffled me was the power of one priest – John Charles McQuaid, Archbishop of Dublin and Primate of Ireland. Though by the time I arrived in Dublin he was "on the way out" as an acquaintance of mine pointed out to me, he seemed to have ruled the Irish Catholics with an iron fist. I was to learn later that he was a master disciplinarian and succeeded in making his flock conform to his puritanical attitude to Catholicism over a long period of 32 years.

Among the older generation in the late-1960s and early-1970s there was total obedience to the teachings of the Church. Somehow, I found it extremely difficult to understand why the Catholics took their religion so seriously, and why they allowed the Church to dominate their lives. Fear of sin permeated through the different classes of Irish Catholics. Therefore, my impression was that whatever the priests preached from the pulpit was accepted as the gospel truth. No questions were asked, no discussions, there was no room for any individual conscience – just attend church without fail, and make sure you go to confession. There were long queues of people outside the confessionals especially before Easter, Christmas and other Holy Days of Obligation. People who attended mass regularly did not automatically walk up to the altar to receive their Holy Communion – they felt they could not receive Communion without being fully prepared or going to confession if they felt they had sinned.

During the late-1960s and early-1970s when I was a student in Trinity College, I was fascinated by the sight of people streaming in and out of Clarendon Street Church in Dublin. That church was always busy with people going in and out to pray, light a candle, say the rosary, attend mass, benediction or go to confession. The doors of the church remained open throughout the day. There were no fears of vandalism or robbery – unlike today. It was convenient for people who either worked in the city, or were there to shop. I admired the strong faith of many Irish Catholics and often wrote about it to my father, who, though born a Hindu, did not believe in running in and out of temples. Of course my father had no equivalent of a Pope or an Archbishop, Bishop or a priest in authority to lay down rules and regulations about the responsibilities and duties of a Hindu. On the other hand, my mother, a devout Hindu, who went to the temple on a regular basis all her life had no problem attending mass in St Anthony's Church or a service in the Methodist Church.

In fact it was my mother who was anxious that I should receive a convent education, and entrusted my childhood to the capable hands of Holy Family Sisters. They certainly educated me well and looking back I am convinced it was because of their quiet influence that I chose – of my own free will and after much deliberation – to become a Catholic when I grew to be an informed adult. Perhaps it is because I am a convert to Christianity, because I was not born into this religion but had to learn and understand the teachings of Christ, that I tend to ask questions, seek explanations and not take my faith for granted. I was very fortunate in that Father John Gildea, a Holy Ghost priest nurtured my faith and gladly gave of his time to discuss various aspects of my faith and the teachings of the Church with me, without any fear or guilt for over 30 years. Therefore, I found it difficult to understand the unquestioning attitude of the Irish Catholics towards their Church and faith.

The more I questioned my Irish Catholic friends out of sheer curiosity about the way they practised their religion and their obsession with the Church, the more I realised that Irish Catholics had a very different attitude towards their Church, compared with many Catholics in other parts of the world, and my own native country in particular. Fear of sin, fear of hell, fear of the priest, or fear of missing mass, fear of going to bed without saying their rosary and prayers seemed to govern their faith in the Lord and their Church. Somehow, as an 'outsider', I did not dare speak my mind on matters about the Catholic Church, though I felt disturbed by the knowledge that fear of sin in particular played a pivotal role in the lives of many Catholics – young and old. As a foreigner, I did not feel I belonged to the Irish Catholic Church nor did I feel it was necessary to follow its strict teachings. I did not believe that it was any of my business to question the apparent strong faith of my friends or acquaintances.

Thirty years on, I see no mantillas, no rosary beads, no queues outside the confessionals, no large crowds of people standing at the entrances to the church during mass on Sundays, all things which were quite common sights in those days. Today, there are more empty seats in the churches, a reduction in the number of masses said on Sundays, noticeable fall in parents with small children attending church – simply stated, in the Ireland of 1998 there seems to be a huge apathy towards religion and the Church. Perhaps people today do not feel controlled by the Church; instead they are in control of their lives, their faith, their spirituality and their obligations. Probably they have had enough discipline imposed upon them by an authoritative Church, or perhaps they are tired of all the scandals surrounding some of the clergy in the Catholic Church and feel cheated. The very people who preached *ad nauseum* about good, Christian and Catholic living and about sin were, all the while, 'sinning' themselves.

As the Church scandals began to unfold, I noticed a deep sense of disappointment and anger towards the Church amongst many of my acquaintances, friends and neighbours. The young in particular found it very difficult to accept that the Bishop who 'sinned' was not dealt with properly and fairly. Was it right to send that Bishop who fell a prey to his biological needs, so deviating from the vow of celibacy, to a developing, poor nation in South America? The questions are many and varied, but I strongly believe that my Christian and Catholic faith should enable me to accept human weaknesses and failings, even of Bishops and priests, and forgive them. Whether they should remain as Bishops or priests is another question!

The Catholic Church is the one topic that often arouses a great deal of anger and emotion, heated debate in my discussions with various Irish people from all walks of life. Even those who are young, and were born in the 1960s, frequently talk about their anger at the Church and the manner in which it has curtailed the normal human development of its flock. Yet talking to the seventeen and eighteen year-olds, the story is different. Some of them just do not bother with the Church, they do not care about the scandals. They feel that the Church is welcome to cater for those who want to be part of it, but they simply do not want to be dictated to, not only by the Church, priests or nuns, but by anyone else either. They feel they are able to make up their minds on how to live, how to be caring, and by and large, they come across as very caring young people. In contrast to this there are other young people who feel the Church has let them down and would like to see the Catholic Church deal with its problems, adopt more democratic methods and shed all the pomposity and authoritarianism.

Why has the Catholic Church earned the opprobrium of so many Irish people? Reading about the late Archbishop John Charles McQuaid gave me some insight into the nation that Ireland was, before I arrived here. It also helped me to understand the reasons for the anger expressed by some people. The intricate linking of the Church and the State, the rules and regulations laid down by the Archbishop, which seldom allowed for any deviation from the teachings and expectations of the all-powerful Irish Catholic Church, denied people choices. It seemed to me that the Archbishop decided what was good and what was bad for his people and the State allowed that to happen.

However, despite all the accusations levelled at the Catholic Church and its teachings, or more precisely the manner in which these teachings were carried out until the late-1960s, the Church has made some valuable contributions to this nation. The foundation for much of the educational and health services were laid by the Church and are still in place today. The increased secularisation of both these services in the recent past has not, to my mind, necessarily improved their quality. This secularisation was made inevitable by a significant change in the Irish society: the inexorable decline in religious vocations.

As I see it, two factors contributed to this decline: foreign television programmes which exposed a hitherto protected population to a wider world outside, and the changing economic situation, which offered a wider choice of careers. Gone were the days when it was considered prestigious to have a son or a daughter enter a seminary or a convent. One had only to glance through the death notices in the newspapers to note the pride of place given to sons or daughters, who were in religious communities when a parent died. Just 25 years ago one could not walk down some streets of Dublin without noticing groups of nuns or priests, but today it is a different story. Even if there are a few of them out and about, their dress code has changed – where have the nuns and priests in 'black' gone? This is no major disaster. In fact the Church has evolved into a Church of the people, for the people – ordinary people – not a preserve of the Archbishops, Bishops, Monsignors, Reverend Fathers or Reverend Sisters. No-one will then deny they too are an intrinsic part of the Church. In the Ireland into which I came, there were no lay readers, there were no altar girls, there were no lay people giving out the Holy Communion. All these happened because of the fall in vocations and of course Vatican II.

The Catholic Church had no alternative but to accept the inevitable need to involve lay people to take on some important tasks of the Church. I believe that the leaders of the Church failed to look ahead and plan well in advance to meet the demands of a changing society. A young priest working in Cork explained to me a few months ago, "The hierarchy just did not keep in touch with the real situation, they simply carried on as if Ireland was still in the 1950s or 1960s, they should have involved the laity much more and much earlier – you do not have to be a priest or a celibate to preach the gospel." Indeed you do not.

Ireland placed the Church and religion on a pedestal and depended too much on them to take on most of the social and educational responsibilities of the nation. The nuns, brothers and the priests carried out those tasks to the best of their ability, but I noticed the beginnings of marked economic, social and political changes in the 1970s, which continued into the 1980s except for a brief period of recession.

Ireland gradually began to free itself from the Church. Newspapers were competing with national television, and the style of reporting news items and other stories became aggressive. The power of the media replaced the power of the Catholic Church. Investigative journalism had no respect for hitherto very 'respectable' individuals in the Church and the State. Some of the worst cases of abuse by certain individuals of the Church and its organisations, be that abuse physical, emotional or the naked abuse of power and trust, were exposed by the media. The media also became the judge and the jury. The Church of the 1990s can neither defend the defenceless nor does it know how to deal with the abusers or apologise. As a consequence, it seems to me that it lost the influence it has exerted over Irish society for all those years.

Was it right to have passed judgement on the actions of the Catholic Church, some of its clergy and the religious organisations from the platform of the 1990s? There is no question that it was right and necessary to have unearthed the truth and exposed the culprits. However, it appears to me that the media failed to discern the truly bad from the truly good. Have we tarred all religious representatives with the same brush and marred their genuine efforts to serve the Church and the society? Should we not salute all those priests, sisters and Christian Brothers who have served this nation well and continue to serve it despite all the scandals caused by the unacceptable behaviour of some individuals in the Church? Thanks must be extended to the media too. Perhaps in a convoluted manner they have enabled the Catholic Church to examine its faults and decide on the kind of contribution it should make to Irish society as it moves into the millennium.

I strongly believe that practising Catholics need guidance from their Church, but not from a smug Church that is unwilling to cater for the changing needs of the society. The silence of the Church and its leaders on crucial social matters during the past year or so is not only puzzling but worrying too. I look forward to a continually evolving Church that can happily involve people of all ages and from all walks of life. The Church should be accountable to its people. Transparency is the name of the game in modern Ireland.

As Ireland moves into the next century, the Catholic Church that was equated with the Ireland into which I arrived, will have to acknowledge and accept without any reservation that there are other religions too. It was most encouraging to read what Father Vincent Twomey of St Patrick's College, Maynooth had to say on this matter: "Indeed there is much to be said for a coming together of the Christian churches, and indeed other religions, to articulate confidently the concerns of Christians and non-Christians alike for a just and moral society . . . Come together they must, if voices for selfishness and elitism are not to prevail." (*The Irish Times*, 15 April 1998.) Ireland, it is said, is on the verge of becoming a multi-cultural and multi-religious society. If that is going to be true, the Catholic Church has an obligation to show by example that Christianity is about tolerance, compassion, compromise and helping all people irrespective of the country from which they originate, the class to which they belong or the faith in which they believe.

In this context, the Church of Ireland, despite being a minority Church with under 100,000 members has managed to remain scandal-free and even become attractive to some middle class Catholics. During the past two decades enormous changes have taken place with more and more Catholics attending Church of Ireland services, and children attending its schools and youth clubs. It is acceptable to be associated with the Church of Ireland. Gone are the days when the Catholics would have been afraid of having anything to do with any Church except their own. Ireland has become more pluralist and there is a closer co-operation between the Catholics and members of other denominations. There is also a growing sense of admiration among those Catholics attracted by the Church of Ireland for its democratic methods, tolerance, respect for individual conscience and equality among all.

The theocratic society advocated by the late Archbishop Charles McQuaid has vanished forever. The Church has suffered a severe body blow and is obviously hurting. It has to dig deep into its own conscience, and undo the damage it has done over the years to the faith of its own flock. Regaining credibility is not going be an easy task. Who knows, modern thinkers and doers in the Church, and surely there must be a few – Dr Willie Walsh, Bishop of Killaloe comes to my mind – given time, may find the answers to bring people back to the pews because that is where the people want to be, rather than because the Church says so.

My dear friend, Cannon Billy Gibbons, a retired Rector, who served all of us, Protestants and Catholics, so well for over 20 years in Kill O' The Grange parish, and who now lives in County Tyrone, never fails to impress upon me that churches of all denominations are suffering – not just the Catholic Church. Should the Catholic Church take consolation in the Rector's view point? Perhaps Ireland has joined the ranks of many other affluent and materialistic nations, and believes that the Irish Pound is almighty God! It could also be that the 'new' Ireland has become a mature sovereign State by effectively tearing away from the apron strings of the Catholic Church. I believe that the mature voice of the Church is necessary particularly in the light of all the cultural changes that have taken place over the past two decades. Not only the Catholic Church, but also all the other Churches must speak with confidence on issues which affect the common good of the society and should have the freedom to do so.

In the final analysis, irrespective of which Church we belong to, we must take responsibility for our own faith, our values, traditions, attitudes and behaviour toward each other and others in society. The Church can only inform and guide us. We must also stop looking back and continuing to blame the Catholic Church and its clergy forever. The media too have a positive role to play and should refrain from demonising the Church. Enough is enough.

The Church, the State and the male politicians for a long time, failed to treat women as important members of Irish society. In the Ireland into which I arrived, their attitude towards women, the status women held in society and the employment opportunities available to them, left a lot to be desired. However, women in many developed nations of the world began to empower themselves during the 1960s and Irish women were not going to be left behind. I have observed through the years and in particular the past ten years, the inexorable rise of women in Irish society. It was no mean achievement. One can only marvel at the way in which women have gradually made a niche for themselves in the commercial world of Ireland today.

Education, equal opportunities in employment, financial independence, availability of contraception, ability and freedom to opt out of difficult marital relationships, have revolutionised the status and role of women in modern Ireland. Women had to fight very hard for the changes in legislation concerning their affairs. It was a long and difficult battle, won in the face of many obstacles over a long period of time, though there is still more to be achieved by women. More women are in full and part-time work in this country than ever before. The direct consequence of more and more women at work has no doubt given enormous satisfaction to women and has also improved the standard of living for many families.

Nevertheless, with all its merits, the inescapable question is, "What is the effect on children when both parents are working outside the home?" Are children growing up to be self-sufficient, independent and well-rounded individuals to face the challenges of the much changed and changing society? Crèches and the pre-schools have become prominent in many cities and towns, and many young children are spending an inordinate amount of time outside their own homes and away from their parents. Highly educated working mothers and fathers tend to spend 'quality time' with their children. Do the children understand and accept that 'quality time' is being given to them? Are the children being 'time-tabled' to react and respond to the valuable time parents allocate to them, after a day's work outside the home?

In the Ireland of the 1960s women stayed at home and took on the responsibility of rearing their children. But times have changed, and therefore, this is not about sending the women back to being barefoot, pregnant and in the kitchen. This is essentially about nurturing the future, ensuring that children and parents make the most of the valuable and irreplaceable precious time between birth and school at least. Therefore, I strongly believe that one working parent, father or mother, once they choose to undertake the huge responsibility and joy of bringing forth a new life into this world should be helped by their employers in every possible way to enjoy parenthood and give of their best to their child.

No two psychologists, sociologists or parents seem to agree on which parent should take on the full-time parenting job at home while the other is at work. There are numerous research papers and books published regularly on this topic. I make no apologies for making perhaps not a very politically correct statement that from my own experience as a mother, who opted out of full-time work outside the home to bring up our child, the gains were many. There were disadvantages too but I can only thank my education, which helped me greatly to keep my mental faculties alert, active and productive. No two cases are the same but children deserve the very best parenting, not just when they are very young, but even as young adults. I was more than surprised when my young daughter having conveyed the impression that she was self-sufficient, independent and well able to handle all her affairs at the age of seventeen telephoned me twice on her first day in college, "I just wanted to hear your voice. I am OK now that I have talked to you." I was glad to be available to her at the other end of the phone.

Though I have all the education and experience necessary to seek and find a job, I have enjoyed working on my own and at home. I hate the idea of losing my freedom and taking on any employment outside my home. The more I hear about what some women at work call 'aggro' in the workplace' the more I am glad and extremely grateful to my parents for endowing me with quality education – education in the quest for knowledge and not just for a specific job. They also encouraged me always to be independent, innovative and utilise and apply my knowledge to anything that I wished to do. In 'recycling' my knowledge I became self-sufficient and in that process motherhood became very enjoyable too. As I see my daughter progress through her life and education I see the positive effects of my input into her early years. I say "Hurrah! this is my life now and I shall move on." Essentially the secret of my own satisfaction and fulfilment as a full-time mother is the direct result of the parental input into my early life, and more importantly I felt liberated in a very conservative society.

Parental care, education and attitude without a shadow of doubt helped me to remain liberated and build on the confidence given to me when I was a child not only by my parents but also the extended family and caring neighbours. In Ireland with more and more grandparents at work, either part-time or full-time, the extended family is fast becoming extinct. The neighbours are often at work too, a totally different scene from the Ireland of ten or fifteen years ago.

Parents do not always know what is best for their children nor are they always fully equipped to handle parenthood. There are no degree courses on parenting. We all strive to make use of our abilities to be good parents. The future of Ireland firmly rests on the children of today and irrespective of their background they should all begin their lives with unconditional love, care, encouragement, self-esteem and equal opportunities. Who better to give them the very best than their parents? Whether it is a two-parent or single-parent family, the most important players are the children. It would be foolish to suggest what works for one family will work for another. Neither is it about full-time mother versus working mother, nor about one making the other feel inadequate or incompetent. It is simply about children. It is the collective responsibility of the parents, the society and the State to ensure the very best for the citizens of tomorrow.

Whatever the attitudes of some people in Ireland of the 1990s to religion, the Church, sex, money and materialism, after 30 years of my life here, I have benefited immensely from some very old values and traditions of this country. I also brought with me a number of traditional values from my own ancient, eastern culture, which I cherish and respect. Today in Ireland, respect for old people, born of the maxim that wisdom came with age, respect for other peoples' property, respect for public property and respect for the environment are beginning to disappear. The rights of the individual seem to be more important than the rights of the community at large. Good basic manners, courtesy and patience have been replaced with aggression, bad language and intolerance – is that progress?

Recently, I have noticed an outright rejection of some wonderful Irish characteristics which have always been major assets: I am constantly aghast when I hear the expletives pouring out of some young drivers caught in traffic jams. I watch with despair as people of all age groups throw their litter on public roads; I agonise as I see young people and children vandalise trees on the roadside for no good reason – I dare not ask them to stop; I listen with no answers when old people in hospitals or nursing homes tell me how the young nurses cheekily address them by their first names without their permission; I get nervous when I hear young politicians argue their points aggressively and without any respect for the age or experience of some of our senior politicians. I feel saddened when I read about the details of payments to politicians and that so many tribunals are necessary to unearth the truth. There are many more examples to illustrate the decline in standards and behaviour of some people in our society today. Whatever has happened to the words 'please' and 'thank you'? Have we simply become obsessed with work, money and power?

Having heard so much about the 'undesirable' features of American and British societies from a number of Irish people, it is interesting to see these features being embraced by some people in Ireland. I am heartened however to note that this is less prevalent among those under 20 and I am hopeful that this rising generation will reverse the trend. Having grown up in an era of relative prosperity they do not see economic growth as the be-all and end-all. They see education and prosperity as conferring obligations rather than rights.

Teachers, policemen, soldiers, priests and above all TDs and government ministers – beware!

Dazzled by the Celtic Tiger, Irish society seems unaware that something, somewhere has gone wrong. For 25 years and more people have been carpet-bombed with the message of individualism. They have been taught that it is not worth sacrificing personal freedom and self-fulfilment for the greater good since the greater good is simply an instrument of social repression.

This had its effect. A growing number of people have come to believe that only fools make personal sacrifices for the common good. When institutions that were specifically dedicated to the service of others and the service of society arrive at this same conclusion then we are in deep trouble.

David Quinn
The Sunday Times, 26 July 1998

COLAISTE DHULAIGH LIBRARY COOLOCK

Chapter 7

Asylum-seekers, Refugees and Racism

> Breathes there the man with soul so dead,
> Who never to himself hath said
> This is my own, my native land!
>
> *Sir Walter Scott*

For a long time Ireland was not perceived as an independent nation in many parts of the world. Those who knew about Ireland thought that she was either part of the British Isles or a poor country in Europe. As recently as 1990, I remember an English receptionist in a London hospital asking me, "Is Dublin in Belfast?" when I gave her my Dublin address.

To many in Asia and Africa, Ireland was only known through the Irish missionaries working in hospitals or schools. In Africa in particular the Irish sisters and priests had spread the good news that Ireland was different – a land of the thousand welcomes, a Christian and mainly Catholic nation. A poor country but basically very different from England, "we are a nation of friendly people, we are a neutral country, we have no imperial past" – that's what I heard not only from the religious people but also many lay people who worked in Nigeria, Kenya, Ghana, Cameroon, Sierra Leone and other African countries, which became independent during the 1960s and 1970s. During the 1950s and 1960s there was also a presence of Irish sisters in some schools and hospitals in some parts of Ceylon, India and Pakistan. While I was revisiting India in January 1998, a young salesman in a shop in Agra in Northern India proudly said, "I was taught by the Irish Christian Brothers, they were just wonderful," when I told him that I live in Ireland. A doctor in Madras, Southern India (whose son, also a doctor, worked in a hospital in Galway in 1995) sang the praises of the Irish people, "I visited your lovely country just two years ago. The Irish are a very kind, helpful, generous and friendly people. I had such a pleasant holiday and I look forward to visiting your country again soon." I found it difficult to share his enthusiasm and wondered would he receive the same welcome in the 'new' Ireland of today?

Ireland's best export to the developing nations from the 1960s to the 1980s was its religious sisters, priests and the Christian Brothers. Whilst many of these dedicated people worked as volunteers and gave of their expertise and time to many countries in Asia and Africa, it is worth noting that a number of them including lay missionaries were also employed by the governments of the countries in which they were working. Therefore, they were paid a salary. Young Irish teachers who worked on contracts in some countries in Africa acknowledged that they were there to save some money towards deposits for their future homes back in Ireland.

For a long time in the history of this independent nation, many other countries in the world – rich as well as poor – opened their doors to many thousands of Irish people on a temporary and permanent basis. The emigrant Irish worked very hard and contributed to the societies in which they were working and also spread the good news of Christ and helped to build a number of churches, schools and hospitals.

From private conversations I had with some Irish missionaries with whom I had the pleasure of working for eighteen months in Nigeria, it was obvious a number of them enjoyed living and working in the developing nations. They liked their freedom away from a very conservative, insular and parochial Irish society. They enjoyed their lifestyle and their privileged, ex-patriate status. It would be foolish to suggest that life and work were in any way easy in the tropics. Very high temperatures, humidity, mosquitoes, cockroaches and other insects, bad roads, poor and crowded public transport, non-availability of good meat and meat products, the lack of fresh milk and other dairy products did not make for an easy or comfortable life. Nevertheless, as missionaries, they were happy and content to adapt to the demands of a tropical life and the native populations were glad to welcome them into their own societies. The expatriate staff had many privileges, and many renewed their contracts and stayed on in some African and Asian countries for many years. Some even opted to take up permanent residence in these countries, and contributed positively to the education, health, economy and life in general.

Therefore, my question is, "Why is the modern Ireland of the 1990s turning its back on people from the poor, troubled nations of the world who are arriving here seeking a safe place in which to live and work?" Foreigners, white and non-white, who came between the 1960s and the 1980s were very few, and by and large were fee-paying students in post-primary boarding schools and third-level colleges. Only a handful of the highly educated, professional people who married into the Irish community stayed on to work mainly in the medical and educational sectors. The Irish did not show any signs of resentment, or racist feelings, nor did they set out to humiliate anyone who had not been born and raised in Ireland.

When my young eight year-old nephew from war-torn Ceylon came to study in Dublin in 1981, one of the officials in Dublin Castle could not have been more helpful. Permission to reside with me and my family in Ireland was granted readily and the official was loud in his praise of my nephew's handsome looks, and sympathised with the fact that a young boy had to be separated from his parents as a result of an on-going conflict between two ethnic communities. Though the same young boy returned to his parents after two and a half years, his education and safety continued to suffer as a result of the escalation in the civil war. Therefore, I was asked by his parents to make arrangements to take him back on a temporary basis. This was in 1990 and much to my surprise, the task of obtaining a visa from the Department of Justice, for his entry into Ireland was neither simple nor easy.

As an Irish citizen, I had lived, worked and paid my taxes in Ireland for 23 years. I was not looking for a permanent residence permit for my nephew. The UK, Germany, France and Canada had opened their doors to some of the Tamil refugees from Ceylon. In the late-1970s, Ireland had welcomed some of the displaced Vietnamese people and helped them to integrate into the community. Therefore, I failed to understand why the Department of Justice was so reluctant to grant a temporary visa for my nephew. I did not ask for financial assistance – born and bred in a community and a family which never depended on government hand-outs or charity, it would have never occurred to me to ask for financial help from Irish society. All that I asked for was a visa for two years so that my nephew could finish his post-primary education.

My pride was hurt, and yet my nephew's safety was of paramount importance. I had no alternative but to plead with the official in charge of sanctioning the visa, having managed to obtain an introduction to him through another official, who happened to be a friend. I made a strong case for my nephew holding back my anger, my tears of sadness and disappointment with a nation I had loved so dearly and lived in for so many years. I was also shattered by the rude, and at times, very aggressive attitude, during my visits, of the Department of

Justice staff, some of them junior, towards the few foreigners who were there to be interviewed for residence permits or to make applications for extending their visas. There were no greetings, no smiles, no friendly words, just harsh looks. There was an arrogant attitude displayed without any embarrassment towards the foreigners. Were the staff in the Department of Justice given special training to deal so harshly with foreigners? I wondered. For the first time in Ireland I became conscious of being a foreigner and felt ill at ease and very inhibited.

I succeeded in getting a visa for my nephew for just two years, but I was most anxious to find out the reasons behind the reluctance of the Department of Justice to issue this temporary visa. I understood from very reliable and informed sources that my nephew's nationality was the major issue. Had he been a white-American, a Western European, a New Zealander or an Australian there would have been no problem. I concluded that if I had not taken out Irish citizenship in the early-1970s, most probably I would have been asked to leave the country or deported. It was too late to deal with coloured people like me who arrived in Ireland years ago, well before the economic boom – the 'Celtic Tiger'.

In contrast to the attitude and behaviour of the government officials in the Department of Justice, the Principal, staff and students of the Christian Brothers School in Monkstown, were kind, courteous and generous to my young nephew. His nationality, colour or creed made no difference. He was a very happy student, very popular at school, and served as a senior prefect. He left Ireland for Canada immediately after his Leaving Certificate examination was over because there was no way he would have been allowed to stay an extra day – this was a condition of his temporary visa. It is worth noting that the Irish tax-payer did not support my nephew. His parents paid for his education and I took care of the rest of his expenses. He was not a 'parasite' on Irish society.

When my nephew, who is now a Canadian citizen, returned to visit us just a year ago he was singled out by the immigration officials at Dublin airport, and this is how he summed it up, "What is wrong with this country? I arrive here on a week's holiday, I have my return air ticket, I have my travellers' cheques, I am a legal citizen of Canada, I carry a Canadian passport and the message was, you are not welcome here." Nevertheless, he had a wonderful holiday, and my neighbours, friends and his old school friends made him feel very welcome. On the day he left for Canada after his holiday, he whispered into my ear, "I wish I could come back to Ireland and set up a business, the quality and pace of life are just great. Do you think they will let me live here?" I did not give him an answer because I was not sure whether he would be welcome here or for that matter whether the Department of Justice would even grant him a residence permit or visa.

Despite having lived and worked in Ireland for so many years I found it difficult to ask for asylum for a single member of my blood family. I would not apply because I refused to beg to the mighty officials in charge in the Department of Justice. Fortunately the rest of my family had no difficulty in obtaining residence in Canada and Australia.

Some Irish people tend to regard an asylum-seeker or refugee as an inferior human being *per se*, totally disregarding – or choosing to remain ignorant of – their backgrounds, education and the politics of repression, which forced them to become refugees. Furthermore, the Irish people must know from their own history how hard they fought for political freedom and human liberties from their colonial masters. How often I have heard the Irish people quoting their own history to me and how much they have suffered at the hands of the British. How often I have been told about the Irish Civil War – brother fighting brother. How often I have been told how much they resented being treated as second class citizens by the English or referred to as a 'Paddy' or an Irish navvy. Jerry Kivlehan OMI of the London Irish Centre explained the hurt, anger and exclusion the Irish emigrants felt on the day they had to leave Ireland. He said, "Being rejected by the 'host country' is part of the experience of most immigrants." (*The Irish Times*, 3 June 1998.) In fact he suggested that: "We are not learning from our own experiences of exclusion and discrimination if we treat immigrants to Ireland in a hostile manner or in the manner that Irish emigrants were treated in the past." This is why I am at a loss to understand why some of the Irish people seem to take pleasure in humiliating the refugees, calling them ugly names and treating them with contempt. I am reminded of Yeats' words:

> Hurrah for revolution and more canon-shot!
> A beggar on horseback lashes a beggar on foot.
> Hurrah for revolution and cannon came again!
> The beggars have changed places, but the
> lash goes on.
>
> *The Great Day*, W B Yeats

One of the basic human instincts is to fight for survival and surely all those harrowing stories and pictures of the Ugandan-Asian refugees in 1972 and the recent Rwandan refugees cannot be forgotten or dismissed by any civilised people who are fortunate enough to live in a democracy and lead a comfortable life in their own native land. The killing fields of Vietnam, the Bosnian massacres and similar atrocities in so many parts of the world speak volumes about man's inhumanity to man. How generously Ireland extended its welcome to members of the Vietnamese and Bosnian communities just a few years ago. How courageously some of the young staff of Dunnes Stores demonstrated their support for the basic human rights of the South African Blacks. What a fitting tribute it was to welcome that South African elder statesman Nelson Mandela, who had been locked away in a prison for 27 long years in his own native land, and make him a Freeman of the city of Dublin. Humanity and Christianity were in full action – I was so proud of my adopted land.

Now that Mr David Andrews, our Minister for Foreign Affairs on behalf of the Irish Government and people, has invited Nelson Mandela to revisit Ireland, the black statesman will of course be extended the very best of Irish welcomes and hospitality when he arrives. And rightly so. Would some of the Dublin politicians and the present Minister for Justice who appear to be against extending the Irish welcome and hospitality to African refugees and asylum-seekers be there to extend that Irish welcome to a black man? If they do, wouldn't that smack of sheer hypocrisy?

There are many in Ireland who will remember the famous speech by the late Martin Luther King, "I have a dream . . . " They will remember his struggle to free his people from the uncivilised and inhuman attitudes, words and barbaric deeds of a majority of the white citizens of America. I do not believe for a moment that the Irish need to be reminded of the importance of human rights, freedom and justice. Irish history cannot be and should not be forgotten in a hurry, simply because Ireland is now enjoying an unprecedented period of prosperity.

Is it not because of the very dire situation of the famine of 1847, and the poverty and unemployment prevalent during the more recent past that there are millions of Irish people living abroad today? Wasn't it the generosity of all the other nations, which made it possible for the 'poor' Irish to escape from the difficulties of life in Ireland? They may not have been refugees, but most certainly were economic migrants and quite a number of them (estimated at 135,000 in January 1988) are illegal immigrants in the USA! Some pundits would have us believe that these Irish migrants were fulfilling a need in the countries to which they were emigrating, when in fact they were escaping the economic hardships in their own land. This is specially true of those who went to America and was eloquently pointed out by Jerry Kivlehan OMI, of the London Irish Centre in Camden Square:

> It is not true to suggest that Irish people emigrated to America or Britain in order to respond to the demands of the labour market in those countries. Most Irish people emigrated because of poverty and economic necessity. They emigrated in order to address their own lack of finance and in so many cases to earn money to send home to reduce the financial distress of the rest of the family. "The letter" from London, New York etc., was an essential source of income into many Irish homes over the past century . . . Money from Irish emigrants has played a significant part in the creation of Ireland today. (*The Irish Times*, 3 June 1998.)

Of course not all those seeking refuge in Ireland are genuine refugees. No-one is arguing that Ireland should embrace and welcome anyone and everyone. Ireland boasts its hospitality and employs the slogan 'Céad míle fáilte' for purposes of promoting tourism in some selected rich and developed countries. Therefore, it would be very naïve to expect the Irish to open their doors and welcome anyone and everyone especially those who are not armed with big chequebooks or bank drafts.

Mary Ellen Synnon was very eloquent when she said, " . . . foreign individuals ought to be let into this country only if they have something specific to trade for the benefit of Ireland". (*Sunday Independent*, 15 February 1998.) She even went further to substantiate this very point, "which is why, eight years ago, I wrote that the Department of Foreign Affairs ought to be in Hong Kong recruiting Chinese businessmen to move here". Mary Ellen Synnon obviously did not see yellow as a colour because her main concern for the 'new' Ireland was, "Ireland, already split by religion, is about to be tinted by colour". (*Sunday Independent*, 15 February 1998.) She also strongly recommended that the immigration officer should escort the 'useless' individuals back on to the boat. I arrived in Ireland 31 years ago without a huge bank balance – did that make me a useless individual? Are all the 200,000 unemployed people on social welfare in Ireland useless people?

If the wealthier nations which opened their doors to the Irish had operated a policy that only 'useful' foreign nationals with something specific to trade for the benefit of their countries would be let in, I wonder how many Irish people could have possibly emigrated in the past?

Only a decade or so ago the Irish government was making a very strong case for increasing the number of US visas available to Irish immigrants. Would the Irish have liked it if the American people failed to be sympathetic towards their plight and repatriated all the illegal Irish immigrants? A mere 5,000 asylum-seekers and refugees have become such an enormous problem to a nation, which for the first time in its history has become wealthy. Mary Robinson, our former president and the United Nations High Commissioner for Human Rights addressing a major forum on human rights in Dublin (organised by the Department of Foreign Affairs to mark the 50th anniversary of the Universal Declaration on Human Rights) said new-found prosperity brought with it "new obligations and responsibilities". (*The Irish Times* 9 March 1998.) She added: "In Celtic Ireland wealth was not measured by what you had but by what you gave." It occurs to me Celtic Ireland, having reaped the benefits of its membership of the EU in abundance, is still not happy or content with what it has received. It wants more and more – perhaps a direct result of prosperity, materialism, and greed is the fear of losing the grip on the new-found wealth.

Why Ireland, which shared its limited resources so generously with the poor, starving and suffering people in many parts of the world as long as I could remember, is not prepared now to open her doors and welcome in some such people, is puzzling especially in the light of the fact that we have more than ever to share with others. Equally disturbing is the silence from the powerful Church leaders and the Catholics in particular – why? Is it because the Church itself is preoccupied with its own issues of scandals, falling attendance at Church services or masses, shortage of priests and nuns and above all the loss of its own long-enjoyed power, authority and influence?

When and how did it all begin? In the summer of 1997, during the general election campaign, a couple of politicians deliberately set out to raise the refugee issue in their bids to be elected to the Dáil. There is no doubt whatsoever that these politicians simply ignited a latent racist flame, and this flame began to spread much faster than any one ever imagined. Loose, insensitive talk, highly exaggerated claims about the huge drain on the economy of the nation, sensational newspaper headlines and reports on the major problems facing the country, many discussions on radio and television programmes followed. People like me – 'outsiders' – who had lived here for a long time without any difficulties became concerned not only for our own future but also for our children, a number of them offspring of mixed parentage (Irish/Asian or Irish/African).

These children are as Irish as any other Irish person, born and bred here, and yet they look different. They know of no other land or home. On one of the television programmes hosted by Derek Davis in the latter part of 1997, a young lady with white and non-white parents spoke of her fears, " I was born here, I have always lived here, this is my home, Dún Laoghaire is my home, please do not make it difficult for people like me." I could not believe that the situation had escalated so rapidly and that this woman had to make such an appeal. A teacher from Cork, Aine Ní Chonail, who was later to found the Immigration Control Platform, was completely unsympathetic. I exclaimed in horror to my own family, "Television – a powerful medium which should serve to send positive information on different races, their culture and the importance of human rights, to everyone, and young children in particular – is it doing enough?".

I felt I had to do something, to say something about this 'new' illness creeping into the Irish society. I chose to go on the radio and make an appeal on behalf of the refugees, asylum-seekers and the minority immigrants. I telephoned the editor of *Morning Ireland* on RTÉ and made a very strong case as to why my viewpoint should be aired. My request was granted and Richard Dowling from the *Morning Ireland* team arrived in my home to interview me. I appealed for restraint in politicians' language, I asked for consideration towards children of mixed marriages, I pleaded for compassion towards genuine refugees and strongly urged that the evil of racism should not be given credibility or even tacit approval, and that every effort be made to nip it in the bud.

The response from those who knew me and who took the trouble to telephone or write to me was most encouraging. "But you are one of us – I never thought you were different." "You belong here. Don't you worry about some silly people's carry on. Sure they have nothing else to do." "What are we going on about? Didn't we go to every corner of the world when things were bad for us?" Richard Dowling telephoned to say the response to the programme was positive and encouraging.

This is the beauty and charm of the Irish. Always ready to extend a friendly reassuring word and welcome to people like me, and it would be such a pity if the Irish were so carried away with the new wealth and new, imported ways of life that they cast off these inherent qualities. There seems to be a new form of 'sophistication' and selfishness in some segments of our society, which I find very difficult to understand.

The attitude of a small but vociferous minority of the Irish people towards the asylum-seekers and refugees is worrying, but what is more worrying is the stance adopted by some journalists and newspapers. I believe it is as a direct result of the media reporting that the 'refugee asylum-seeker' issue became in the words of Andy Pollak of *The Irish Times*, "much more volatile and potentially dangerous". I have, for many years, felt fully involved in Irish life, I have even been able to forget that I am Asian and a foreigner. However, in the very short space of twelve months, things have changed. As a result of the reports by some powerful people in the media and the attitude of some Irish people towards foreigners, refugees and asylum-seekers, I now feel inhibited, scared, sad and am always wondering about my sense of belonging in this society and where my next port of call may be!

Though refugees have been arriving in Ireland for a while, at least since the Irish economic situation improved, people did not take much notice of them. The same was true when a small number of government sponsored refugees from Chile arrived in the 1970s, and from Vietnam and Iran in the 1980s. People in areas such as Blanchardstown, were extremely sympathetic to the Vietnamese boat people and were most keen to help them settle into Irish society – which they did.

Father Michael Mac Grill, the Jesuit sociologist and author of the 1977 work *Prejudice and Tolerance in Ireland* updated his study just two years ago and reported that there had been "a significant and substantial decrease in racism" since 1976. He suggested that this was in part due to black role models such as Nelson Mandela, Paul McGrath, the soccer hero and Phil Lynott, the rock musician. "Up to a few years ago the overwhelming consensus was that people found racism both abhorrent and alien to the Irish world view." (Pollak, 21 February 1998.) This is not true anymore, a fact illustrated by various reports in the newspapers, some from as long ago as 1995:

April 1995 *The Irish Independent* carried the story of a Jamaican couple being driven out of their Dublin city flat.

May 1995 *The Sunday Independent* carried a feature on "the growing levels of racism in Dublin and quoted the revulsion of residents of the building where

> the Jamaicans had been living; the condemnations of local councillors; the opinions of an official of the Council for Overseas Students; and the conclusions of Father Mac Grill."

Though the reporting in the newspapers was somewhat sporadic up to 1997 ugly reports about the alarmingly rapid increase in the number of asylum-seekers began to appear regularly from April 1997 (Pollak, 21 February 1998.) Not all the national newspapers embarked on sensationalist or one-sided negative reporting on the refugee issue. In an editorial on 18 April 1997 *The Irish Times* alerted us to the need to keep a sense of proportion about the "supposed immigration problem". It stated clearly: "The State is not about to be over-run by a tidal wave of foreigners who will undermine the daily fabric of our lives. Compared to any of our EU partners, we are dealing with scarcely more than a trickle of immigration. Ireland still has fewer – far fewer – asylum-seekers than most other European countries. If nothing else, the current phenomenon only serves to underline how we have conspicuously failed to take our fair share of refugees and asylum-seekers in the past."

However, other newspapers did not heed such sensible words and reading some of the headlines and the reports on the refugee asylum-seeker issue left me very worried. On 5 May 1997 *The Irish Independent* urged me to "open my eyes" – a famous advertisement for the newspaper – and read about "Gardai move on dole fraud day trip refugees". The story beneath that sensationalist headline was that at least two dozen Nigerians and Algerians were travelling from Britain, sometimes daily, to fraudulently claim thousands of pounds every week. Gardai and government officials were quoted as investigating "foreign criminals posing as refugees and claiming welfare benefits". Surely such reporting must have damaged the cause of the genuine refugees in the eyes of the Irish public. Defrauding of the welfare system by citizens of many countries is nothing new. No hard-working and conscientious tax-payer likes to see the welfare system manipulated and abused by their own citizens or foreign nationals pretending to be refugees. Therefore, I can understand to an extent the anger and resentment of the Irish people towards refugees caused by *The Irish Independent* story.

However, I was forced to question the agenda of *The Irish Independent* behind such a one-sided and provocative feature. It appeared to me that the newspaper was determined to whip up anti-refugee, asylum-seeker, foreigner, immigrant feelings amongst its readers. How could a responsible newspaper adopt an irresponsible and unnecessarily sensationalist attitude to its reporting of a very delicate and important human issue that concerns all of us? Human fear about the 'unknown' is natural, irrespective of where people live. To capitalise on that 'fear' of the Irish towards the 'outsiders' arriving in Dublin or elsewhere in the country, and drawing attention to, at times, unsubstantiated and exaggerated negative stories about the refugees and asylum-seekers was, to say the least, calculated mischief on the part of the newspaper.

My increasing fear and worry about the refugee issue becoming more and more explosive was confirmed by many more newspaper headlines and reports which followed in the ensuing months: "Inmates lobby to stay in jail as refugees fill up hotels." (*The Irish Independent*, 13 May 1997.) Though the story was in the main about serious overcrowding in Mountjoy's female prison, it managed to state in the second paragraph: "Efforts to reduce over-crowding through temporary release have merely resulted in some women prisoners lobbying to stay in jail because foreign asylum-seekers were being given preference on hostel places, leaving nowhere for prisoners to go when they are freed." Once again the aim of the story was to heap the blame on the asylum-seekers for prison over-crowding and pressure on homeless accommodation.

For many years I have heard and read so much about the poor, the disadvantaged and the homeless and about the inadequate funding for suitable accommodation for the homeless in Ireland. On 1 January 1988 – ten years ago, and well before the refugees and asylum-seekers arrived on the scene – there was a call in *The Irish Times* for the government to allocate £1 million to end youth homelessness. Yet all of a sudden there is a new-found concern for the poor people of our society from unexpected quarters, and the refugees and asylum-seekers stand accused of yet another crime in addition to 'defrauding' the welfare system.

Fintan O'Toole, of *The Irish Times* wrote quite succinctly, about the "rather sickening sight of people who never gave a tuppeny damn for the homeless and the poor suddenly discovering them. The cry goes up that this influx of economic migrants is taking resources that rightly belong to our very own poor people". Have the Irish forgotten that there were many Irish people in the UK before and after it joined the EU taking the resources that belonged to the poor there? I recall a conversation with a post office staff member in Britain in 1985: "You know the poor Irish arrive here with so many children, the Catholic Church advises them to have more and more, and we pay out an enormous amount of money as children's allowance every month."

The headlines and stories about refugees and asylum-seekers continued with great vigour. Take for example a headline in *The Sunday World* on 25 May 1997: "5,000 refugees flooding into Ireland" and the contents of the story underneath: "Many are paying out big money for false passports provided by ruthless gangs of criminals in mainland Europe. The immigrant flood is costing Ireland millions, with the State forking out up to £100 a night to provide some refugees with hotel beds." As if all this was not enough to provoke anger, fear and hatred towards the refugees amongst its readers, the same paper had a double-page spread inside with the sub-heading: "Floodgates open as a new army of poor swamp the country."

Up until this point in time *The Irish Times*, (a newspaper I have read since 1967 and considered to be sensible and usually judicious in its coverage of sensitive topics) had refrained from aping the other newspapers with regard to refugees and racism. Paul Cullen, the paper's specialist on this topic, who later won a 'European Year against Racism' prize for his coverage of the issue, kept the readers well informed on refugees and asylum-seekers without panic-inducing hysterical headlines. However, on 26 May 1997 the paper carried a full page of articles by its security correspondent with frightening headlines that read: "Influx of asylum-seekers causes concern", "Dublin now main target for gangs trafficking in people", "Shopkeepers say theft by Romanians is snowballing." Immediately afterwards, I heard my acquaintances who work in the city complain bitterly about the aggressive Romanian beggars, "Where did these people come from?" "We do not want these people annoying us", "Dublin is not used to beggars."

How did the genuine refugees and asylum-seekers feel about the newspaper headlines and reports? Did they notice any change in the attitude of Irish people towards them on the streets and in their neighbourhood? I discussed the effects with some refugees and asylum-seekers, "We do not understand why they are writing so many bad things about us?", "We are subjected to racial abuse, verbal, and at times physical, on the streets in the city", "Two old men asked me to clear out of here very fast or they will . . . ", "We are afraid to go out and the politicians are making it very hard for us", "The Irish nuns and priests never told us the Irish were racist." So the comments continued.

I noticed a great fear and sadness amongst those refugees to whom I talked. One African woman feared for her young children, "Six months ago we had no problem, people in the neighbourhood were so welcoming and suddenly I sense their hostility – why? 'Go back to your jungle' they say." I simply had no answers. I found the whole situation worrying. Surely this cannot be true of Ireland. I have lived here so long and never experienced any hostility. I telephoned a few of my immigrant friends who, like me had made Ireland their home to ask whether they or their children were experiencing any racism. No, they had not. One of my friends said, "I have become very conscious of being a foreigner living here of late and I am worried for my children." I responded, "I feel the same."

Within a few days the powerful words of Fintan O'Toole in *The Irish Times* about the "breathtaking hypocrisy" of the Irish, gave me some hope that a certain balance was being injected into the newspaper reporting about the illegal economic immigrants, asylum-seekers, refugees and racism issue. He took our memory back to 1989 when 44,000 Irish people emigrated and wrote, "we went through a paroxysm of national outrage at the plight of illegal economic migrants in America. We buttonholed every senator and congressman with an eye on the Irish vote and expressed our sense of betrayal at America's refusal to accept as many of our economic refugees as we chose to send her".

After reading Fintan O'Toole's sensible words, I wondered whether some day in the future Irish politicians would woo the votes of today's refugees and asylum-seekers to get elected to the Dáil. As a legal immigrant of the 1960s and a legitimate citizen of this nation I felt very proud to be invited to go on the general election campaign trail with a politician in the early-1980s. Prospective voters at the door were more than happy to discuss political issues with me and found time for pleasant jokes about politicians. Soon after Dr Bhamjee from Clare was elected to the Dáil in 1993, I was invited by a political party to be a candidate at the following general election. The question today is, "Would people like Dr Bhamjee, or even me, put ourselves forward as candidates, win seats to the Dáil or elsewhere if there was a general election in Ireland tomorrow?"

But *The Irish Independent* was determined to continue with its mission of frightening its native Irish readers about the refugees and declared on 31 May 1997: "Tax-payers to face bills of £20 million plus for refugee flood." Soon afterwards the headlines in *The Evening Herald* screamed that the refugees were getting £20 million pounds in welfare payouts. The very next day *The Irish Independent* came up with a front-page headline: "Crackdown on 2,000 'sponger' refugees." "The Department of

Justice clampdown comes amid fears of a huge influx of immigrants attracted here by the country's generous welfare payments," the article stated.

The truth is that just one Romanian refugee had been deported and yet the article quoted some security officials estimating that "in the longer term . . . between two and three thousand refugees will be turned down for asylum and sent back to their home countries". Of course this was a deliberate attempt to frighten the asylum-seekers. The alarming headlines continued to appear in some of the newspapers for another month or so even after the general election. "Refugee flood to spark home crisis, report warns", "Refugees 'flooding' maternity hospitals". The most extreme of all the headlines appeared in one of the tabloid papers, *The Star* on 13 June 1997: "Refugee Rapists on the Rampage" and went on to point the finger at the Romanians and Somalis. What chance had the refugees amidst all these mostly unsubstantiated claims? Is there no-one to speak on their behalf? I became more and more concerned not only for the refugees and asylum-seekers but also for immigrants like myself who have lived here for many years.

I felt very scared too because I could very well be the target of verbal and physical abuse. Simply speaking I would not have known how to handle such abusive and volatile situations. I advised my daughter to be extra careful and not to get involved in any sort of discussion relating to the refugees with any native Irish person, who may very well be racist. Yet my daughter is a native Irish person. Her father is a native Dubliner. I am the foreigner! Since I travel in and out of England on a regular basis in the course of my work, I became very nervous as I disembarked in Dublin for fear I could be singled out by the immigration officials and made to feel embarrassed. I became obsessed with my Irish passport – I refuse to leave home without it. Thus far I have escaped any difficulty or embarrassment despite the irresponsible whipping up of racism by certain politicians and newspapers. The strange fact is irrespective of which airport I have arrived at in England – Heathrow, Birmingham, Stansted, Manchester – over the past few years, I have never been asked to produce my passport. On the contrary, because of the frequency with which I travel to the UK, some of the airport staff have got to know me and always find a minute or two to exchange a few kind words with me.

Towards the end of June 1997, the Irish committee for the European Year against Racism stepped in with a press conference to articulate their horror about the newspaper coverage of the refugee issue. The Irish co-ordinator, Philip Watt, said some of the coverage "can at best be described as irresponsible and at worst as outright racist in content". Though he did acknowledge that the balanced and well-researched reports were "undermined by the application of an alarmist or sensationalised headline or sub-heading". Some papers especially *The Irish Independent* chose to ignore the press conference.

Of all the print space given over to an extremely sensitive refugee issue throughout 1997, the most painful, hurtful and frankly thoughtless words were those of a north Dublin TD – he wanted the "rogue" asylum-seekers, who were "carrying on in a culture that is not akin to Irish culture" quoting begging and "bleeding of lambs in the back garden" as examples, to be "kicked out" of Ireland. He went on to say: "There is such resentment about this in the inner city that I'm concerned that there will be a serious outbreak of violence of some kind." He even claimed that Ireland has a higher proportion of asylum-seekers than most European countries – this is untrue! The statistics for 1996 show the following: Germany took 149,193, the UK, 34,800, The Netherlands 22,170, France 17,405 and Denmark took 5,896, while 1,179 refugees were taken in by Ireland. Amazingly no-one in authority or with power challenged the TD's words.

However, it would be foolish to think that if this matter of asylum-seekers, refugees or illegal economic immigrants or the racist attitude of some Irish people is kept away from public discussion that all will be well. In a democratic society freedom of speech and freedom of the press are essential. All of us may not agree with what we have to say to each other or write about matters concerning some difficult human issues with which we are faced, but it is healthy to speak our minds in a sensible and calm way. We all have our prejudices – some are explicable, some are not. Most are borne out of fear of the unknown and "incomplete education" as Senator Joe O'Toole, General Secretary of the Irish National Teachers' Organisation explained in an interview on the radio.

An Irish woman married to an Algerian for twelve years explained, "We like to think we are generous and welcoming, we like to hear how good we are, how welcoming we are, it is simply that we pretend we are holy Catholics and we are happy to say 'welcome' to outsiders without meaning a word of it, we are damn hypocrites." She was ostracised by her family for marrying an Algerian. Her own mother, sisters and brothers had refused her husband and children a welcome. There must be many Irish women and men in similar situations. Nevertheless, from my experience of living here for a long number of years, I also know of many families that have extended a very warm welcome to their non-native daughters and sons-in-law.

How did my Asian family react to my marriage to an Irishman? This is a question, which needs an answer too. My mother just could not, and would not, accept my husband. For three long years I battled with her to recognise my marriage to a Dubliner and she refused. Let us look at the reasons for her refusal: "How could you bring such shame to your family? What will the neighbours and our relations have to say about your foreign white husband? Do you realise that no decent young man or woman in our own community would wish to marry into our family? We are not beef-eating people, we are not drinking people – our morals and values are much higher than those people in the West, how can you possibly disgrace our family?" So she went on week after week, in her lengthy letters to me. She was also most concerned that I had chosen a man whom as she put it was "not our class", despite the fact that she had never even met my husband or his family.

Finally, after numerous letters and phone calls to my mother, when I went over on my own to see my parents and the rest of my family to assure them that there was nothing wrong with my inter-racial, inter-cultural and even inter-religious marriage (I hailed from a very orthodox Hindu family), a large circle of friends, neighbours and relations of my Eastern family did not welcome me back or talk to me. As far as they were concerned I had simply let down a whole community of my people by marrying a 'foreigner', an 'outsider', a 'stranger' and a white man. They were so sure that children borne of this inter-racial marriage would never belong in the East or the West. My mother went even further to say: "What about the children? Do you realise they could be red-haired and brown-skinned and probably end up as alcoholics? How would they fit into the Irish society or our society? Would they be accepted as individuals? How can you be so selfish?" The same old story – fear of the unknown.

The truth is, my mother and people in my native country were very ill-informed, very ignorant and very intolerant. I confess I was disappointed with my educated mother – a teacher. I would have been asked the same questions if my husband was Indian, African, Japanese or even a Ceylonese from a different caste or creed. I recalled how a young girl in my parents' neighbourhood committed suicide because her parents would not allow her to marry the boy she loved – the reason being, he was from a lower caste than her family. Such stupidity! I felt very sad and angry that a precious young life was crushed forever as a consequence of racism and gross stupidity.

On a rational level I could understand how my family felt about my Irish husband, and I knew, over a period of time and with patient reasoning I would succeed in getting my mother to accept my husband, which I have done. The red carpet was rolled out for him when I brought him to meet my family. Garlands of flowers, baskets of fresh pineapples, mangoes, limes, mangostens and rambuttans, different varieties of bananas and every possible tropical vegetable, specially milled and polished white long grain rice and Orange Pekoe tea – the champagne of Ceylon – all of these things were waiting for him. My uncle employed special Moslem chefs to cook meat dishes and deserts so that his nephew-in-law would not go hungry. I was amused. There were times I felt neglected by my parents because they were so busy taking care of their son-in-law. The family barber was so thrilled that he could arrive each morning to give my husband a shave. The washerman was so pleased that he could wash and iron the clothes and my husband was delighted to be part of my Eastern family. At my mother's request my husband and I went to the temple and the priest was happy to welcome us.

Ignorance of each other's culture makes people fearful, and it is this fear which is readily exploited by those looking for scapegoats to cover their own inadequacies. Hitler's scapegoating of the Jews has been well-documented, so it is disappointing to see present-day politicians indulging in similar tactics. At the same time, it is interesting to note that with the exception of a courageous few, the main bulk of TDs and senators have hardly made any positive statement on the refugee, asylum-seeker issue.

It is quite likely that racist feelings have always been present in Irish society, as in any other society, but as long as there was no likelihood of people of different races coming to live here these sentiments could be indulged, and even excused as the ravings of madmen. Now, however, it is a different story. Even if those who express these sentiments do nothing more than that, there is a danger of less mature, more impressionable minds being influenced to indulge in acts of violence against immigrants. It is not enough for politicians to wring their hands. If they do not support the expression of racist sentiment (and I fear some of them may), then, they must legislate against it.

In December 1997, at the closing ceremony of the European Year against Racism in Luxembourg, the Declaration of Intent 'Europe Against Racism' was published. It was interesting to note that under the Declaration, main signatories from all Member States of the EU confirmed the fundamental rights of people to live free of discrimination and harassment on the basis of race, colour, religion or national or ethnic origin. Current government ministers, former government ministers and representatives from the four pillars of Social Partnership in Ireland are the key Irish signatories to the Declaration which encourages us to "take part in the process of European mobilisation launched through the European Year Against Racism; We call upon all European Institutions, public authorities, private organisations and individuals at both European, national and local level, to contribute in everyday life, at school, at the workplace, in the media to struggle against racism, xenophobia and anti-Semitism".. Impressive words indeed, but words and signatures are not enough. For that matter even proper legislation against racism is not enough. Ultimately people will have to accept each other with all the differences and similarities – be these differences, physical, cultural, religious or anything else.

An editorial in *The Irish Times* in September 1997 said there was a very powerful and constructive message about the refugee debate being "as much about us as the asylum-seekers who increasingly want to come here. What kind of Ireland do we want for the new millennium? Is it to be a multi-cultural society? If so, how is this inclusiveness to be achieved? Discussion of these [issues] has hardly begun."

We must have discussions and we must have them now, and they must take place on an on-going basis. There are no ready-made answers or quick solutions to the 'new' problem of refugees and asylum-seekers facing the nation. There is also the question of economic migrants. As Andy Pollak said in his address to Cleraun Media Conference on 21 February 1998: ". . . we are at a sensitive moment in an Irish society which is trying to come to terms with the difficult, rapid but exciting changes brought about by an unprecedented level of prosperity and a relatively new outward-looking involvement with a multi-cultural Europe." Indeed the changes are exciting and changes are inevitable in a modern fast-moving world. Weren't the changes brought about by our European membership followed by prosperity that is attracting people from other nations to make their way here?

Ireland has a rich heritage and culture. Many Irish emigrants through the years have brought with them their own culture and shared it with many other nationalities all over the world. If our emigrants could adapt to their lives in other multi-cultural societies, notably the UK and USA, we, in Ireland, should be able to accommodate the foreigners who are arriving here and their culture. It may not come naturally or easily to a nation that has up to recently managed to maintain its own monoculture. However, there is always the first time. Ireland has a lot to learn from other countries that are used to foreigners arriving as immigrants, refugees or asylum-seekers. Rules, regulations and government procedures are of course necessary, but, the most important element in the refugee debate has to be information and education. Not just informing and educating the asylum-seekers or others who may be economic migrants, but also the Irish people themselves. If the newspapers had concentrated more on the positive aspects of handling the refugee issue, I believe racism would not have surfaced so quickly. Now that racism has become a major issue and there is no point denying it, the first step is to try and find ways it can be combated.

All humans share a fear of the unknown. It is this fear among the refugees which makes them stay together in a given area. The refugees also have no choice in the matter of accommodation or where they live. The authorities place them in certain areas where suitable accommodation is available. (Quite a few Irish landlords have quickly converted available buildings to rent them out to the refugees and asylum-seekers with the intention of making a tidy profit.) And it is not that they set out to intimidate the native people on a road or in an estate of houses. The refugees themselves derive a sense of security by clustering together – as such clusters tend to proliferate and become mini-ghettos in the long run. It is very easy to say that refugees must be dispersed or distributed among the Irish people in different parts of the city, county or country towns. Until such time as the refugees are allowed to work, and begin to trust the native population (and be trusted by them), and are in a position to move freely and choose where they wish to live, there will always be difficulties.

How can we, the native population, help to build that trust between the refugees and ourselves in the short term? Recently on a radio programme an Irish woman said, "I am tired of saying 'Good morning' to the two African gentlemen who live down our road." From my own experience of people in Africa, they are cheerful and chatty by nature. I can only guess that the two gentlemen the lady referred to were most probably afraid of revealing their identity. Could it be the fear of being reported to the Garda? Could it be a language problem?

Whatever it is, people who come into Ireland will have to be helped to understand and learn our language, our culture, in short, our way of doing things. Equally desirable is for us, the natives, to learn from other nationalities about their culture, their way of life and even make an effort to learn their languages. Learning any language takes time and even when the language is learned, it can take even longer to master the art of conversation. Take one example, "May I please have that book?" A foreigner whose mother tongue is not English may simply phrase it, "Give me that book." without meaning to be rude or arrogant, but most probably translating it from his or her own language. There are colloquialisms too – when I say to my English friends, "I am grand, Thank you" or "You are very bold" they simply have no idea what I mean. Therefore I try and find alternative words: "I am very well, Thank you" and "You are naughty." I am fortunate to be able to find alternative words and phrases but we cannot and should not expect our 'newcomers' to be fluent in English or acquire a wealth of vocabulary in such a short space of time. We will have to be patient with them. After all these years of living in Ireland I have not managed to master the Irish language, a fact that makes me feel thoroughly ashamed.

My research shows that apart from some English language classes in the city there are no facilitation centres for refugees to meet and get to know each other and local native people on a social level. In getting to know the native people the refugees and asylum-seekers will have an opportunity to equip themselves with ways and means of coping with the Irish culture. Perhaps the Irish Refugee Council or the Vietnamese Association or other similar national voluntary organisations and local churches could help to invite small groups of refugees and Irish people on a regular basis to meet and simply chat over a cup of tea or coffee. No formal talks, lectures or classes – just informal gatherings where people can relax and get to know each other's culture.

What happens if there is no common language? I remember an occasion when I had to spend an evening with a group of Japanese gardeners who spoke only a few words of English. I speak no Japanese at all. We managed without too much difficulty because the giggles, smiles and laughter of the Japanese ladies helped me to relax and communicate with them. Our hands and the eyes took over from our tongues. The secret behind that successful evening was the fact that there was no fear of meeting strangers. The hosts, an Englishman and his wife, made every effort to help their guests relax and enjoy themselves without any fuss.

It is true that refugees are in a different and difficult situation to those Japanese visitors, and the uncertainty of their future in a foreign land automatically inhibits them from being themselves. Perhaps the Irish people with their smiles can make them feel welcome and help them to relax and communicate with each other. Preconceived ideas about foreigners or prejudices against their speech or deeds or assuming our way of doing things or behaving is the only, right way, or is a better way are bound to cause difficulties when meeting other nationalities. A little perseverance, patience, tolerance and understanding will go a long way to make the get-togethers reasonably successful.

Culinary evenings may be another way of getting to know the eating habits and food preferences of other nationalities as well as introducing them to our food. Music is another common link between different nationalities. Perhaps musical evenings with singsongs would help break any barriers between 'us and them'. Church and school appeals to native families to play host to an asylum-seeker may be another way of welcoming, informing, educating and exchanging cultural values. There are three and a half million Irish people and only 5,678 (as of 1998) refugees and asylum-seekers. Surely there must be quite a number of Irish families with open minds and hearts to make a refugee or asylum-seeker feel welcome.

The purpose of the different types of social get-togethers is not only to help the host nation to overcome the prejudices, at times inexplicable and innate, towards others with different culture, but also to facilitate learning and understanding of each other's way of life. This is not easy, but with a bit of effort on both sides, it can be done. The number of refugees and asylum-seekers are still relatively small. If we do not make that effort and go an extra mile, to include the newcomers in our society and help them embrace some of our cultural values and traditions it will be very difficult to even consider the possibilities of a multi-cultural society in Ireland.

While there is a great deal of concern among many responsible and caring Irish people and organisations about how Ireland should deal with the issue of racism, as an immigrant I have no doubt that educating the native Irish and the immigrants about the positive aspects of multi-culturalism is absolutely vital and is essentially the only way forward. Yet, I despair. Some of the national newspapers continue to frighten and alienate the Irish from the refugees and asylum-seekers. Well known radio voices continue to make alarming noises about refugees and asylum-seekers. Why?

Education: a long term solution?

The world may be divided into continents but there is only one species of man. Yet there is variety. Different races of human beings, different physical features and skin colour, different languages, religions, traditions, values and cultures will always be there. People in different nations and continents have over the years crossed and continue to cross the geographical boundaries. The reality is, more and more human societies have become and are becoming multi-racial, multi-religious and multi-cultural. Like it or not, Europe is multi-cultural and Ireland is part of Europe. Ireland though a small island nation, cannot close its doors and continue to exist as a mono-cultural society. The only way forward is to be positive and constructive about the new situation in which we find ourselves with regard to the refugees, asylum-seekers and economic immigrants. We must consider integration and a positive policy of inclusion, and we must hope for a pluralistic society. Perhaps the first step towards integration lies in assessing our own reasons for various prejudices against people, especially foreigners, and then embarking on ways and means to educate and inform newcomers about Ireland, its people, places, culture, heritage and so on without attempting to make them feel inadequate or inferior.

Pre-schools and primary schools should be the starting point, and educating the very young should be the priority in this refugee debate and discussion. Edna O'Brien, in an interview she gave a very long time ago, talked about the different colours of the flowers – all combining beautifully together to present a pretty picture in the garden but at the same time retaining their individuality. Dr Mohamed Al-Sad'r, spokesman of the refugee community in Ireland said in an interview at the beginning of 1998, "It is only through nipping racism in the bud early, and through education, understanding, dialogue and admitting mistakes when they are made that Ireland can be a safe home for all its white, black, yellow, red, Protestant, Catholic, Jewish and Muslim people." So, let there be no doubt that our children will have to be taught about race, colour and religion from a very early age, if Ireland is to become a 'safe home' for everyone in the new millennium. Children do not set out to be racist in their attitude towards those who are different from them. They have to be taught to be racist and often pick up the attitudes of their parents and relatives towards the 'outsiders'.

You've got to be taught to hate and fear
You've got to be taught from year to year
It's got to be drummed in your dear little ear
You've got to be carefully taught

You've got to be taught to be afraid
Of people whose eyes are oddly made
And people whose skin is a different shade
You've got to be carefully taught

You've got to be taught before it's too late
Before you are six or seven or eight
To hate all the people your relatives hate
You've got to be carefully taught.

South Pacific

South Pacific is a celebrated musical, written 37 years ago. It is not just a musical about war or about World War II. In the words of Theodore S Chapin, "It dealt with a theme which was to become a major preoccupation of the decades to follow: racial prejudice."

Nine years ago a little Chinese girl who was adopted by Irish parents in my neighbourhood, saw me working in my garden one summer day and without any inhibition said, "I know you, you are brown because you were born in a very sunny country. Weren't you? I am yellow because my real daddy is Chinese I think. Do you think China is not as hot as the country you were born in?" Obviously her adoptive parents had taught her to accept people who look different from her with the right attitude. She even knew the reasons for the differences in skin colour. A photograph in *The Irish Times* on 8 April 1998 featured three very happy and proud Irish adoptive mothers holding their Chinese infants in their arms. Those children, my little Chinese friend who is a teenager now, my young adult daughter and many other young people of today who are "not completely Irish or white" have changed the face of Ireland, well before many refugees and asylum-seekers arrived on our soil.

Integrated education may be the stepping stone towards making Ireland a safe home for all the different nationalities that have arrived here. Ireland is also fortunate in that the policy makers and educators have the opportunity to learn from the mistakes made by other Western nations which are already multi-cultural, and put in place a suitable programme of study for our children. There cannot be room for teachers with racial prejudices in our classrooms. Therefore, teachers will have to be trained to deal with children of different nationalities with different cultures, languages and religions. This will not an easy task but with the positive attitudes and tireless efforts from the teachers, parents and other citizens in the society, multiculturalism in Ireland is possible.

From my experience of teaching Asian and African children, I know that most of them hunger for education and it was encouraging to hear Senator Joe O'Toole, quoting the principal of a national school in Ennis in an interview on the RTÉ radio news on 3 June 1998 when he said that "immigrant children are intelligent, receptive, anxious to learn and to adapt". Equally I was heartened to hear a friend of mine, a hard-working businessman say, "We must allow the refugees and asylum-seekers to work and I know they will in no time show us what hard work is all about. They will be an asset to our nation."

There are no guarantees that all the doom and gloom about today's refugees, asylum-seekers and economic immigrants will be replaced by happiness and hope, smiles and laughter, but for the sake of all of us, the native Irish people and the newcomers, we must work together conscientiously to achieve a multi-cultural society. Ireland has many things of which she should be very proud and one of the most striking features I became conscious of during my early years of living here was the fact that a largely Catholic nation had Protestant presidents, such as the late Mr Douglas Hyde and Mr Erskine Childers. Having watched and followed the events in Northern Ireland over a period of 25 years, I firmly believe that the Republic of Ireland has the ability to embrace every race, religion and culture and move proudly into the new millennium.

If the Catholic Church dominated the lives of many Irish people for a long time, so did the problems of Northern Ireland. Ireland has demonstrated its maturity by dealing with Articles 2 and 3 in the Constitution, to promote peace in Northern Ireland. At last there is a ray of hope for both the communities in the North. There are a number of divided communities and countries in the world (including my land of birth) that can and should learn from the Irish example to resolve their difficulties and differences and work towards peace.

Ireland is now faced with the new problem of accepting refugees and asylum-seekers. How mature and well prepared is Ireland to deal with these few immigrants, refugees and asylum-seekers? I deliberately state 'few' because contrary to the much publicised stories about the huge influx of refugees, just 462 people were granted refugee status between 1992 and 1997.

A mere drop in the ocean for a nation that is riding high on a new wave of prosperity. Though there are currently 3,883 applications for asylum that still remain to be processed, it is highly unlikely that refugees will engulf Ireland, despite what some newspapers would have us believe. As I understand it, stringent measures are being put in place to ensure that Ireland's 'welcoming' portals will not be flung open to the refugees, asylum-seekers or economic immigrants from now on. Our present Minister for Justice, Mr O'Donoghue seems determined to close every gap in that 'welcoming' door. However, I hope that he would also ensure that those who have applied for asylum or refugee status and succeed in gaining it would not end up as the pariahs of our society.

If we are prepared to change the words of an Article in our constitution to reflect modern Ireland's readiness to work towards peace in Northern Ireland, I believe those words should also serve their purpose fully of all her citizens including those 'outsiders' who have been granted or who will be granted asylum. I am a legitimate citizen of this nation and have been so for well over 25 years. I cherish my citizenship, I am proud of my adopted land and I well and truly belong here. I strongly agree with Oliver O'Connor, an investment funds specialist, who stated, "Some refugees, asylum-seekers and immigrants are a gift of intellectual capital, which simply arrives free of charge at our national doorstep. We would be mad to ignore it. Others contribute by setting up small businesses. Others will do what jobs they can. In total, they are very few in numbers. We have much to gain and nothing to lose from managing our small diversity well." (*The Irish Times* 13 March 1998.)

Perhaps by managing that cultural diversity well, we may even find some more Paul McGraths for our national football team, wonderful athletes or tennis players and excellent musicians. Would it not be foolish to reject them all? It was heartening to read Roddy Doyle's article 'Thank you Paul' in the weekend supplement of *The Irish Times* (16 May 1998): "'Paul McGrath' was the answer to the following questions: Who is your favourite player? Who is the best player ever to play for Ireland? Who is God? If you were a fertile woman who would you choose to father your children?" Considering that many thousands of Irish people over the years have contributed to the economic and social development of other nations in the world, because they were absorbed into the mainstream workforce, or, through their own initiative, involvement and enterprise, it should not prove to be too difficult for Ireland to grab the opportunity that has come its way for a change. If we have the capacity to give of our best to other nations with joy, then here is an opportunity to take something back, with equal joy and gratitude.

It would be foolish to assume that a non-native, white, black, brown or yellow person because of his or her refugee or immigrant status is devoid of cerebral, social or other human attributes and close the Irish door forever. It is nonsensical to claim as some do that the mono-cultural nature of Ireland should be preserved at all costs. How can we? Ireland is part of Europe and most European countries are multi-cultural. Are we going to constantly stop and embarrass legal non-white citizens from Ireland, Northern Ireland, Britain or other parts of Europe at the various Irish ports of entry to make sure they are not refugees or they are not trying to enter the country illegally? Are we sending out clear but flawed messages that non-white tourists, business people and students are not welcome here?

Fear of 'ghettos' of refugees, asylum-seekers or economic immigrants and non-Irish beggars, combined with fear and resentment of Irish jobs and houses being taken up by the 'outsiders' came across as the main reasons for racist attitudes when I interviewed a number of Irish people during the past year. Another point that was made was that some refugees are 'arrogant' and talk too much about their rights and demand a great deal. Clearly some of the misconceptions about the refugees are the direct result of a lack of awareness about their different cultures but more importantly about International Human Rights. Education and information over a period of time may help to eradicate some of the myths people have about the refugees. Why didn't the Minister for Justice, Mr O'Donoghue and his Department inform the general public that refugees are not allowed to work in Ireland? Why didn't the government and the media inform the public about our international obligations to the refugees and asylum-seekers and highlight their basic rights?

The media reporting on refugees and asylum-seekers more often than not has been very negative and at times has been disturbingly so. What is also worrying and disquieting is the attitude and behaviour of some Irish people in authority towards the African refugees and immigrants in particular.

During my interviews with various Irish people in the past year I identified a sense of 'racial superiority' among a very small minority, "We are Irish, we are Europeans, we went out and 'civilised' some of the dreadfully poor African nations from which these refugees are arriving into our own country. They will never belong here." No amount of information and education can eradicate such intrinsic and hardened views which some people hold. People holding such opinions can be found in any community in any country. However, every effort must be made not to let those views, or undesirable actions emanating from such views, remain unchallenged or harm the innocent refugees, asylum-seekers or economic immigrants.

Often the problems and undesirable effects of multiculturalism in other parts of the world are quoted as a justification for Ireland not going down the same road. Are we not capable of examining the positive elements of a multi-cultural society, accommodating the genuine refugees and granting asylum to those whose lives would be endangered if they were deported to the land from where they came? Another question that is seldom raised is, "Do the refugees wish to return to their native lands when and if normality returns?" My conversation with a random sample of refugees clearly indicated that they would like to return to their countries as soon as it is possible. Some well-educated people found it painful that they were treated very badly by the authorities and were anxious to explain that they were here as refugees or asylum-seekers, and not out of personal choice. In fact they had no choice at all. One doctor explained, "Beggars cannot be choosers. Your whole confidence as a person, as a human being is not there any more because some people treat you with contempt."

One group of people who find themselves in a very difficult position as a result of increasing racism, are legitimate fee-paying overseas students, foreign doctors in hospitals and other naturalised Irish citizens who have lived here for many years, and who have contributed greatly to the economy of the nation. Before the arrival of the refugees and asylum-seekers in Ireland these people were automatically accepted for who they were, but now they too are often identified as 'undesirable' individuals or aliens and are subjected to racism. It is incredible that in a short space of time the attitude of some of the Irish people towards 'outsiders' who are different from them, should have changed, and yet it is difficult to explain the reasons for it. Time and time again 'fear' of what will happen to the major cities and Ireland as a whole if we accept the refugees and asylum-seekers from Africa in particular emerged as a reason for racism. In short, it is about not wishing to have a black neighbour – if that is not about some Irish people proclaiming their 'racial' supremacy, what is, I wonder! A more worrying trend is the emergence of racist, anti-immigrant groups such as "Reclaim Dublin" publishing violent anti-black propaganda under the slogan "Keep Ireland green and white". And also the appearance of racist graffiti and flyers in areas where the asylum-seekers are being housed. (*Sunday Tribune*, 12 July 1998.)

Roddy Doyle's words on Paul McGrath are worth recalling: "He grew up black in a country that is famously tolerant, as long as you're white and Irish and not too Protestant." (*The Irish Times*, 16 May 1998.)

The more I analyse the pros and cons of racism and all the other difficult issues surrounding the refugees and asylum seekers and *bona fide* immigrants, the more I am convinced that the Department of Justice and the Minister in charge have to accept a lot of responsibility for the current situation. The scare-mongering that went on during the past eighteen months, the absence of suitable structures to handle, speedily and efficiently, the applications from asylum-seekers, the negative media reporting, the absence of guidance and statements from the Church along with little or no political will to legislate, have all compounded the whole issue of refugees and asylum-seekers.

At the launch of the Irish co-ordinating committee of the European Year against Racism in 1997, the Minister for Justice, Mr O'Donoghue said the rise in expressions of racism was "a matter of considerable concern and regret to all responsible people". He announced that a consultative committee on racism and inter-culturalism has been established to advise the government on matters relating to racism. This is to be welcomed and it would be desirable, even essential, that the committee (chaired by Dr Crickley of NUI Maynooth), invite views and opinions from immigrants who have made Ireland their homes for a long number of years, as well as from representatives of the refugees and asylum-seekers. Time and time again one of the mistakes many organisations closely involved with missionary or charity work in developing nations made (and I saw them being made when I was in Nigeria), was to formulate policies and actions, however well intended, for the recipients without the full understanding of their culture and traditions. Getting to know their culture could very well be the first step in understanding the 'outsiders' who are the unfortunate victims of racism. Perhaps this is wishful thinking on my part – as an immigrant.

How sincere and committed Mr O'Donoghue and his colleagues in the Government are to deal with the very important issue of immigration, refugees and asylum-seekers, and legislate speedily remains to be seen. The Refugee Act was passed in June 1996 but it was not implemented. Instead on 15 April 1998, *The Irish Times* reported that Mr O'Donoghue was drafting new legislation with stiffer penalties for trafficking in refugees and for employing illegal immigrants, and was considering limiting access to Irish citizenship. Almost a month later the newspapers carried the latest episode in this on-going saga about refugees and legislation. The Government is to introduce new legislation on immigration and residence permits, its main aim being to curb the ability of 'bogus' asylum-seekers and refugees to avail of the welfare system. As Carol Coulter of *The Irish Times* wrote on 20 May 1998: "None of the proposals to have come from the Government over the past two years has reflected the concerns of international human rights organisations or local groups working with the refugees."

As the Government continues to dither about legislation, racism is on the rise. It is also disturbing that the International Convention on the Elimination of all Forms of Racial Discrimination (see Appendix 3) was adopted on 21 December 1965 by the General Assembly of the United Nations and ratified by 150 countries world-wide, including all Member States of the EU, except Ireland. This does not of course mean there is no racial discrimination in all of those countries but it is clear that some effort is being made by these governments to combat racism.

There are no easy solutions to the very complex human problem of refugees, asylum-seekers, immigrants and racism in Ireland. It is all too easy to place the blame on ignorance, fear, selfishness, latent racism that is now surfacing and even the new found prosperity of this nation.

Research in other countries has shown that immigrants in any wealthy Western nation, particularly those from poorer parts of the world, suffer more from racially motivated attacks during periods of recession or high unemployment. Therefore, are we to conclude that the prosperous modern 'new' Ireland has selfishly chosen to turn a blind eye to the less fortunate refugees who have arrived here – no doubt because of the very prosperity Ireland is enjoying? Do some Irish people believe that it is adequate to throw a few thousand pounds into the coffers of the poor nations to alleviate any hardships and poverty ("Penny for the black babies"), and to fulfil their international obligations, and keep Ireland for the Irish? Perhaps not, because Ireland is famous for its compassion, kindness and generosity towards the poor. I cannot see the Irish attitude towards unfortunate people in their own land or elsewhere changing simply because of the nation's prosperity.

The question is why haven't we heard any strong condemnation of the ugly racism from the elected leaders of this society? A few non-committal statements here and there from some politicians are not just enough. Those who were quick to spread all the negative aspects of the refugees were not challenged, or taken to task by those who had the authority to do so. Why? I can only conclude that it is very much a case of apathy towards the immigrants. Perhaps an Irish solution to an Irish problem? The problem might just go away. Perhaps the 'bullies' who are going around attacking innocent black people are being given a passport by those in authority to continue bullying refugees. Perhaps the victims of racism would get more and more frightened for their own safety and move on to another place, another country or even return to their own country to face potentially disastrous consequences. How many of the bullies who attack and cause grievous bodily harm to the refugees have been arrested or dealt with? The Garda have warned refugees not to go out at night for their own safety.

Of course the refugees and their problems are not a priority item on the agenda of the Government, after all Ireland has not felt it necessary, important or urgent to ratify the UN Convention on the Elimination of all forms of Racial Discrimination, which was put in place 33 years ago!

On the other hand, the refugees and asylum-seekers ought to thank Ms Aine Ní Chonaill, PRO, Immigration Control Platform, for her attitude towards them. Judging by the reaction of many Irish people to her stand against immigration, she has not only become a pariah in her own nation, but has raised the level of compassion and consideration of the majority of Irish people towards those displaced from other nations.

However, the revelation in *The Irish Independent* on 19 May 1998 ("Up to one and a half million immigrants are moving towards Western Europe . . .") would be manna from heaven to the Immigration Control Platform and would let its supporters shout: "Don't let them in. Keep Ireland for the Irish" so enabling them to work on the fears of the Irish people. It must be pointed out that the report originated in Germany where the extreme right wing – the German counterpart to Le Pen's Front Nationale in France – has seen a surge in popularity. A senior, very able and moderate politician explained to me, "We are only a small nation on the perimeter of Western Europe – I cannot see even 2,000 such Romanians, Russians, Turks and Albanians finally making it to our shores. Even if they arrive they would not want to stay here because their big dream is to make their way to North America or Canada. We shouldn't get over-excited."

It seems to me the whole problem of refugees and asylum-seekers has become a political and media football. It is a no-win situation. In any democratic nation, freedom of speech is the right of its citizens. For all the ranting and ravings of the late Enoch Powell the 'rivers of blood' never came to pass in Britain, though of course, there were many difficulties including racial riots.

It never fails to amaze me how issues such as abortion or divorce gets our self-appointed moral guardians to be so vocal and full of action as if all the other citizens of this country do not have the legitimate concern for the welfare of the society. Anyone who expresses another viewpoint with some consideration and understanding is categorised as being 'soft' on such important national issues or far too liberal. Ms Aine Ní Chonnail is the self-appointed guardian of our anti-immigration policy. The Government and a large majority of the Irish people will have a rough ride in times to come – perhaps much sooner than one would imagine, if suitable measures are not put in place to safeguard the basic human rights of refugees, asylum-seekers and other immigrants.

If the Minister for Justice Mr O'Donoghue and his Department wish to help the genuine refugees, then they must deal with all the applications as speedily as possible and not just make announcements about their policies or proposed legislation for public consumption. Some of the ill-chosen, ill-worded and unhelpful announcements made during the past year, and especially in recent months, along with some of the media headlines and reporting have in my opinion inflamed and exacerbated the issue of racism in our society.

Let us stop blaming the refugees and asylum-seekers for the ills in our society and help those who are already here. Let us not close our doors permanently to 'genuine' refugees and asylum-seekers in the future by putting in place draconian and inflexible immigration rules and regulations. Some controls are, of course, necessary and no-one could possibly argue otherwise. However, I would ask that consideration be given to the following suggestions which I believe would aid both refugees and asylum-seekers, as well as the nation itself.

- An information desk at the ports of entry manned by well trained, politely-spoken immigration officials assisted by a psychologist and a naturalised immigrant like myself. These people would be trained to extend a welcoming, friendly greeting to refugees and asylum-seekers. The Department of Justice should call upon the services of immigrants, translators (possibly drawn from the refugees and asylum-seekers already granted residence) and psychologists and train them to assist with its work in granting legal status to the people who arrive here.

- Lay voluntary and religious groups, such as The Irish Countrywomen's Association or the Mothers' Union (Church of Ireland), could be encouraged and funded by the government to organise reception-information centres for refugees and asylum-seekers in cities or towns. These centres could organise short orientation courses for refugees and asylum-seekers to help them learn about the Irish culture, traditions and ways of life.
- Lone women and children, unaccompanied minors and the elderly should be accorded priority status and every assistance be given to them, including short-term accommodation in suitable hostels run by experienced staff.
- Youth, athletic and sports organisations should be advised to welcome the young and unaccompanied minors and involve them in the various activities of the clubs etc.

I believe that the refugees and asylum-seekers also have an obligation to do their best to understand the requirements of their 'host country' and adapt as much as they can to make it easy for the relevant officials and voluntary groups to help them. I also believe that the governments of the many nations from which the refugees originate are primarily responsible for their citizens. Poverty, starvation and disease, along with the lack of education, proper hospitals or healthcare and medicines, as well as the extreme weather conditions and drought, are some of the factors which contribute to the enormous difficulties facing developing nations. However, civil wars, military coups, dictatorships, bribery, corruption and personal greed of those in power over the years in the relatively young democracies, also continue to plague these nations.

How can governments who willingly accept international aid to help their countries and citizens then proceed to spend huge sums of money on arms and warfare? If not for the tireless work of international aid agencies and their personnel and the generosity of many people in the developed countries over the years, millions of innocent people would have died. Year after year more and more aid is needed. Many thousands of people, particularly in some African countries, continue to live in the most appalling conditions or end up as refugees in neighbouring poor countries. If only there were speedy solutions to the numerous problems that face some of the developing nations!

Of all the countless number of suffering people in the developing nations, only those few who have the resources manage to find their way out of the misery to arrive in the Western world, some never arrive at their destinations and some arrive dead.

In my opinion the time has come for the leaders and governments of the developing nations and other war-torn countries to reassess their priorities and execute their responsibilities towards their people. However, the rich nations of the world and their people have a human responsibility towards the poor people of the developing countries, they cannot and should not shy away from sharing whatever they can to help the poor.

Western nations and their governments cannot sanction aid to the developing countries on the one hand and make money on the other by selling arms and ammunition to the same nations. This trade will have to stop if there is to be an end to all the conflicts and deliberate mass killings among various ethnic groups and tribes. It is imperative that poor nations in the world make a much greater effort to help their own citizens retain their human dignity. Why should they have to flee from their own lands and be humiliated by those in the First World? To borrow the words of Margaret Sweeney, a member of the Galway Traveller Support Group, it's time some of the developing nations "got their act together"!

She had to make that appeal to her travelling community after being attacked by a gang. It seems to me the whole world is suffering from making politically-correct statements on almost every issue. It is high time all of us, whether in developed or developing nations, take responsibility for ourselves and our actions. The 21st century is just around the corner and with all the scientific, technological and industrial advances and the information explosion, it is beyond belief that there should be so much human misery, poverty, starvation and homelessness in the world. Considering the natural disasters over which mankind has no control, the time has come for controlling and eliminating deliberate man-made ones. The very religions – Christianity, Hinduism, Buddhism and Islam – seem to have taught us very little about accepting each other as human beings irrespective of who we are, where we live or where we came from, and learning to live in harmony. Self appointed 'do-gooders' with their own extreme view points in every society always manage to influence the weak, the vulnerable and the poor.

Moving into the new millennium one can only hope that there will be a roof over every human head, every mouth will be fed and that homelessness and starvation will be a thing of the past. The developed and developing nations must work together to achieve that goal.

It seems that finally the British, 50 long years after the arrival of the first 500 black Jamaicans in London, and after decades of trouble such as the Notting Hill riots of 1958, the Brixton riots of 1981 and a great amount of pain and suffering, mainly as result of discrimination and racism, are learning to live with multi-culturalism. It is an extraordinary schooling for a nation that was once the heart of an empire and is now on the periphery of Europe and is an excellent example of the mistakes which must be avoided. Are we prepared to let "'Ni Chonnailism" take hold and set us back 50 years on the road to multi-culturalism. Ireland, "which has exploited the EU with Gaelic skill and is in the midst of [an] economic boom of mouth-watering proportions" (according to an editorial in *The Sunday Times* of 7 June 1998), has the ability to exploit the intellectual and other skills of our 'newcomers' and learn to live with the difference.

Quotations from Andy Pollak are from his address to Cleraun Media Conference, 21 February 1998.

Quotations on the issue of the status of, and Irish attitude towards, refugees and asylum-seekers in Ireland

---

Dáil Debate, 19 October 1995

The status of refugees is an issue which should strike a chord with every man, woman and child here who has any grasp of Irish history, our history-books being littered with the names and deeds of those driven from our country out of fear of persecution.

John O'Donoghue, TD

The Irish Times, 9 March 1998

. . . an attitude of mind that we are enriched in Ireland by those who come from other countries.

Mrs Mary Robinson,
UN High Commissioner for Refugees

Each of us must promote a generous and positive welcome for the refugee community in Ireland and see it for what it is: as an opportunity for Ireland to develop our diversity and tolerance of difference.

Ms Liz O'Donnell,
Minister of State for Foreign Affairs

Ireland is part of the global village. That's not just a sharing of markets, or a sharing of Tiger economies, it's a sharing of people. Ireland must assume the same responsibility faced by all industrialised countries.

Ms Hope Hanlon, representative for Britain and
Ireland from the UN High Commission for Refugees
(UNHCR)

The Irish Times, 11 March 1998

The costs associated with social welfare, housing, education, health care, employment, etc., for this number of people – which could be of the order of £200 million to £350 million per annum – must also be borne in mind.

Mr O'Donoghue
Minister for Justice, Equality & Law Reform

The myth of Ireland being swamped by refugees is just that, a myth, but it is one that has engendered revulsion and hatred and one that has been used in inflammatory terms by at least one Fianna Fáil member of this House.

They have not come here out of choice but out of necessity.

Ms Liz Mcmanus TD,
Democratic Left

The Irish Times, 16 March 1998

. . . Ireland is our communal home and no amount of wealth makes it everyone's home.

Ms Aine Ni Chonaill, PRO
Immigration Control Platform

The Irish Times, 20 March 1998

With our experiences in Northern Ireland, we, of all nations, should appreciate how racism destroys lives and communities. Through education and example we must root out this social evil before our children come to accept it as normal.

Mr Paul Weir
(Letters Page)

The Irish Times, 27 March 1998

Immigration is, and always has been, a great source of energy, ambition, and innovation for any society. I know, for instance, of teachers in Dublin who now get down on their knees and pray to God for more immigrants. When they hear of the flood-tide of foreigners flowing over the Emerald Isle, they say: 'If only...' They dream of entire classes made up of Romanians and Cubans, Ukrainians and Ghanaians.

When senior politicians like John O'Donoghue can pluck wild figures from the air and insist that they represent the cost of a piece of simple humanity like granting an amnesty to asylum-seekers, it will always be easier to play on fears than to encourage hopes.

Mr Fintan O'Toole
Columnist

The Irish Times, 27 January 1998

May I take this opportunity to say one thing to the political and economic refugees arriving daily on our shores. Welcome!

Dermot O'Shea
(Letters Page)

The Irish Times, 6 February 1998

According to Focus Point (1997 survey) the most significant causes of homelessness are family violence, abuse and rows – not refugees . . . So why this new-found interest, by those opposed to the refugee influx, in a problem which has existed for at least 30 years? And why the sudden explanation of the problem in terms of refugee numbers?

Adrian M Kelly
(Letters Page)

The Irish Times, 13 March 1998

Some refugees, asylum-seekers and immigrants are a gift of intellectual capital which simply arrives free of charge at our national doorstep. We would be mad to ignore it.

Oliver O'Connor

The Irish Times, 4 June 1998

There is a resistance to change in our society and there is a ready market for racism. For this reason we must also address methods of preparing our pupils for a multi-cultural community.

Senator Joe O'Toole,
General Secretary,
Irish National Teachers' Organisation

The Government and all of us have a moral responsibility to respond to the special needs of refugee children and other ethnic minorities. There is enrichment in diversity and we are not talking about charity, but a moral obligation to cherish all children equally.

Dr Willie Walsh
Bishop of Killaloe

The Irish Times, 7 July 1998

The called me monkey, they called me nigger. They pushed me around and then kicked me to the ground. When one of them showed a knife I screamed and they ran off.

Noel Makoko
Congolese asylum-seeker
who was set upon by eight men

Everywhere I go I am insulted. A man slaps me at the bus stop. Someone throws a used nappy at me from his window. The policeman sees it but he does nothing. Truly, this is a hard place to live in.

Land Vey
Asylum-seeker

The refugee issue is a global challenge with a local impact. It's not enough for those of us in government to simply deplore racism; we also have to see to it that measures are taken to counter it.

Liz O'Donnell
Minister of State for Foreign Affairs

The Irish Times, 8 July 1998

Dublin is a multi-racial city – albeit on a small scale. There are horrifying reports of racist behaviour and intolerance . . . Some of this is due to the lack of preparation by State agencies and the voluntary sector in educating both the migrant and settled communities to co-exist.

Gay Mitchell, TD

The Irish Times, 18 July 1998

Sectarian diatribes, some by elected representatives, inspire vile deeds such as the fatal arson attack in Ballymoney. Racist words could do the same here. We have read of refugees and immigrants burnt to death in other countries. I will continue to ask that we should treat non-nationals here as we have asked that our nationals should be treated in other countries.

Senator Mary Henry, MD

The Irish Times, 30 July 1998

So a refugee from Sierra Leone is sent from pillar to post. So what?

Anthony M Cooney
Letters page

The Irish Times, 7 August 1998

A nation stands on its own feet when it has some clear sense of where it has come from and where it's going, when it's not afraid of its own reality. What we have at the moment is, on the contrary, a hysterical denial of Irish experience and a fantastic illusion that the current boom represents some kind of eternal normality, as if we had all grown up knowing how much

Javanese to mix with the Kenyan for a perfect cup of coffee.

Could it be that the hysteria about Romanian migrants comes, not from a sense of their exotic strangeness but from a recognition of their terrible familiarity?

Fintan O'Toole
Columnist

Sunday Independent, 9 August 1998

It is not racist to oppose multi-culturalism.

Mary Ellen Synon

The Irish Times, 10 August 1998

As regards *Lebensraum*, whatever the intellectual origins of the word, as advocated and practised by the Germans it meant invading the territory of others; not holding on to your own. It is, therefore, far more applicable to the immigrant invasion than to our perfectly natural wish to keep our country to ourselves.

Aine Ní Chonaill
PRO, Immigration Control Platform

The Irish Times, 12 August 1998

Of course, there would be problems of racism and of ghettoisation if a relatively sizeable 'influx' were not permitted. But whose fault would they be? And if we treated these immigrants fairly and decently they could enrich this monoglot society, bringing variation to our culture, our style, our language and our mentality.

Vincent Browne

The Irish Times, 13 August 1998

It really is 'a bit Irish' for people to argue that immigrants are taking the homes that rightfully belong to 'our' homeless people. This argument sickens me. Where was all this concern for Irish homeless people before the present so-called crisis?

Each of us needs to have the opportunity to put ourselves in another's shoes, to experience for one day what it is like to be an asylum-seeker. Maybe then we would all be a bit more open and more just, a bit more generous and a lot less ignorant, a lot less judgmental and self-righteous.

Sr Stanislaus Kennedy
President, Focus Ireland

The Sunday Business Post, 16 August 1998

I don't care what nationality, class or lifestyle they come from. They are all non-nationals and there is no room for more. A scattering of exotica is fun; it brightens up our lives. But the days when it is limited are long past.

Aine Ní Chonaill
PRO, Immigration Control Platform

Whether Aine Ní Chonaill and her followers will become a serious political force is a moot point. But, given the reaction from some quarters to recent arrivals in Wexford and elsewhere, it is clear that while few would publicly support her stance, a greater number of people privately agree with her sentiments than would publicly admit it.

Declan Walsh
Columnist

. . . we might at a pinch – spend one extra penny in every £10 of public expenditure on refugee services. Some crisis that, for one of the 20 richest countries in the world.

And let nobody speak out – in government or in opposition – because refugees are only a fit subject for polite conversation if they're ours, and if they're landing on someone else's shore.

Fergus Finlay

Chapter 8

Northern Ireland: 1968–1998

When I arrived in Dublin in 1967, I had absolutely no knowledge of the 32 counties, 26 counties or 6 counties – I just knew I was in Ireland. Then I met a young lady in Trinity College who said she had come from Magee College in Derry and that it was in Northern Ireland. That is when I became curious and over a period of time came to know about Northern Ireland.

Gradually I realised that those students from Northern Ireland who came to study in Trinity College were, in the main, Protestants and that they considered themselves to be British. Though I became quite friendly with two or three students from Northern Ireland, we seldom discussed the political, economical or social aspects of their country. Then one Saturday morning in December 1967 I was at the GPO buying stamps when a gentleman approached me and asked, "Would you have a Free State six pence?" I distinctly remember saying to him, "I only have an Irish six pence and you are welcome to it." He took it, thanked me profusely and went away to make his phone call. As I walked back to the bus stop outside Clery's in O'Connell Street, I kept repeating 'Free State six pence', and wondering why he asked me for a Free State six pence and not just six pence?

The following Monday morning I made arrangements to meet my friend from Enniskillen in the coffee bar just to find out more about the 'Free State six pence'. My friend was highly amused about my curiosity but explained to me about the 26 county Republic known as the Free State and the 6 county Northern Ireland, which is governed by the British. The penny dropped.

I also learned more about the two communities in Northern Ireland, their religions and their ethos. Naïve as I was, I simply accepted that in effect there were two separate countries in Ireland – the Republic of Ireland and Northern Ireland. Between 1967 and 1968 I made one day trip to Belfast at the invitation of another friend of mine from Dublin. He said to me, "I have to get a triptyque to go across the border into Northern Ireland." Noting the surprise and ignorance written all over my face he proceeded to explain, "Oh, a triptyque is a customs permit. I have to get it to bring my car into the Northern Ireland." I had a pleasant trip to Belfast and observed the customs checks on both sides of the border. Spending a day in the shops in Belfast I could not help noticing that things were much cheaper there than in Dublin. Later on I was to learn smuggling across the border from the North was quite common. Another thing I noticed was that people in Belfast were very reserved compared to the people in Dublin. Not many smiles or laughter – they seemed to be quite serious.

Once again in my ignorance I concluded two countries, two different people but failed to understand fully the history behind the division of one island into two separate entities. Determined to become better informed I set about reading books on Irish history and slowly began to understand the whys and the hows. I was taught British history and constitution when I was fourteen years-old but that did not mean I grasped the knowledge needed to analyse and understand British history. Similarly just reading everything about the history of Ireland did not equip me fully to explore and understand comprehensively the problems of Northern Ireland. Yet I knew for certain that all was not well between the two communities in the North.

Deep down I became aware that there were some parallels between my own Tamil community in Ceylon and the Nationalist community in Northern Ireland. I knew, from my personal experiences in my own native land, what it was to be a member of the minority community and how painful it was not be treated as a citizen with equal rights by the majority community. Somehow I felt inhibited to discuss the politics of Northern Ireland or my own country with my Irish friends and acquaintances. I realised as a foreign student and a 'temporary' resident in Dublin that it would not be prudent to air any of my views on the politics of Ireland – North or South. However, I remained quietly very interested in the politics of the North; as a minority Tamil in Ceylon, it was only natural that I would be.

Around the same time I was also deeply concerned about the problems in South Africa. I just could not understand why human beings in some societies found it difficult to live together and be civil and courteous towards one other. I was very impressed with the life led by the minority Protestants in a predominantly Catholic Ireland. They held influential positions in political, academic, commercial and other sectors of the Irish society. They had their own churches, hospitals, schools, their own teacher training college and in a manner of speaking Trinity College was theirs too. I saw no signs of any discrimination against them and concluded that it is possible for people with different religious beliefs to live in harmony. "Why can't the two communities in Northern Ireland or for that matter my own country take a leaf from the Republic of Ireland?" I wrote to my parents towards the end of 1967.

I was not aware at the time I wrote to my parents that the Civil Rights Campaign by the Catholic community was beginning to gather momentum in Northern Ireland. Troubles began in 1968 after the police broke up a civil rights demonstration. Two names left an impression on me. One was Bernadette Devlin and the other John Hume. I kept in touch with events in Northern Ireland through the newspapers, radio and television. The British army was sent into Northern Ireland in 1969 and I remember how the Catholic community welcomed the British soldiers because they really believed that they were there to protect them. Alas! came Bloody Sunday in 1972, fourteen people died after the army opened fire. Everything changed. Soon afterwards Stormont parliament was abolished and there was direct rule from Westminster.

I became aware of the IRA, Sinn Fein, Loyalists, Unionists, UVF, LVF paramilitaries etc. The topic of Northern Ireland seemed too complex and often provoked anger in some people. There was so much hatred, so much bigotry and no trust between the people of the two communities – where was Christianity? I did not dare discuss any aspect of the Northern Ireland problem with any one I knew in Ireland until 27 August 1979, after hearing the news of Lord Mountbatten's murder by the IRA on the radio. Many people in my neighbourhood were horrified by the news and some openly expressed their sadness and embarrassment to me.

Throughout the last 29 years, since the day of the Civil Rights March, there have been so many bombs, so many deaths and so much destruction to property not only in the whole island of Ireland but also in the UK. Politicians in the North, South and UK have worked tirelessly and with commitment to bring about a settlement to resolve the Northern Ireland problem. Two agreements, Sunningdale and Hillsborough had failed. Hope prevailed despite all the difficulties and obstacles. In September 1997, another round of the peace process began in great earnest. Some people in Ireland and the UK became cynical and indifferent to the deteriorating situation in Northern Ireland. "If South Africa can do it why cannot they do it in the North?" asked an English friend of mine – that was in November 1997. On Good Friday, 10 April 1998, the US Senator, George Mitchell, chairman of the Northern Ireland Peace talks declared, "I am pleased to announce that the two governments and the political parties of Northern Ireland have reached agreement." I am only sad Gordon Wilson, a truly Christian gentleman, who lost his young daughter Marie in the Enniskillen bombing was not there to hear those words. They would have been music to his ears.

The agreement included cross-border bodies, an assembly and an end to the Republic of Ireland's territorial claim to the North. 'Yes' or 'No' for the agreement depended heavily on the voters in the Republic and Northern Ireland. I have no doubt more prayers were said during the weeks before the referendum for a 'Yes' vote on both sides of the border. Almost everyone I talked to wanted peace, peace, peace! Thirty years of violence – a whole generation and even the beginning of another, knew nothing but violence in Northern Ireland.

I waited impatiently for 22 May, referendum day, to cast my vote proudly and say 'Yes' to the agreement. As I waited, I failed to understand the intransigence of some Unionist politicians in the North and was even scared that their arguments for a 'No' vote might have disastrous effects on the outcome of the referendum result for which many people were hoping. I even wished the media would go into hibernation and refrain from analysing and re-analysing every word uttered by the politicians, "Why can't the media give us a bit of peace and time to think for ourselves?" I thought, all the time hoping and praying that the result of the referendum would be a resounding 'Yes'.

That memorable Friday arrived, and I made sure to arrive at the polling station clutching my Irish passport and the all important polling card, for fear I might be turned away. Having cast my vote in the affirmative, I found it impossible to concentrate on anything until the results were announced – I wanted a huge 'Yes' vote. And I got it. Ireland got it. Mary Holland of *The Irish Times* (25 May 1998) got it to perfection with her powerful words: "Yes, Yes, Yes – to peace, to politics, to the future." I could not wait to race back to England to tell my English friend, "We did it, We did it, and did it with panache."

The peace process was severely challenged by the bomb in Omagh, which claimed 29 innocent lives and seriously injured many others on Saturday, 15 August 1998. However, the response of the Irish people across the political divide has reaffirmed my belief that permanent peace is possible.

As I rejoice for Northern Ireland and her people, I also hope and pray that the two communities in Ceylon, will reach an agreement to live in peace and harmony.

Chapter 9

Into the Millennium: Aoife Toomey

Ireland has changed a great deal since my mother's arrival here but while she seems to feel that we, as a nation, have lost a great deal during the metamorphosis from small peripheral nation to dynamic and progressive European partner, I believe that more good than bad has resulted. My generation are really the first European children of Ireland, we have always known our country as part of the European Community and in the course of our growing up have witnessed this membership becoming increasingly more social as well as economic and political. We, in Dublin, live in a European capital, a fact that has become even more obvious since the beginning of this decade.

The 1990s have, I feel, seen many radical changes occur in this country, changes more profound for the astonishing speed with which they have happened. A week was said to have been a long time in politics, now it seems that a day is even longer for many aspects of society. Perhaps one of the biggest changes to make itself felt is the lessening of the Church's grip on society. As young people we do not feel its influence that much, we have shed the 'Catholic Guilt' that haunted many of our parents, we no longer live in fear of sin or condemnation from the Church. One of the reasons for that I think is that the media has taken over many of the guidance roles previously allocated to the Church. Many of us feel that the Church has failed to move with the times and as a result its teachings lack relevance and understanding of life in the 1990s. Consequently we look to the media, which is not only up-to-date but show us things beyond our limited national horizons, it broadens our perspectives and our opinions, shedding light on lifestyles and customs about which we previously knew nothing. The media is also not there to preach but to inform, something that makes it very appealing to us.

The Ireland that has changed so much is one very much made for the young and the young at heart; there does seem to be a growing sense of isolation among the more elderly in our society, who find it difficult to cope with the speed of change or the changes themselves. However while my mother might feel the loss of our 'Irishness', we feel we have gained enormously in self-identity over the last ten years. Ireland is no longer a country dominated by the Church or overshadowed by Britain. Rather we have come into our own, in social and economic terms, to take our place on the world stage. We are no longer the poor member of the EC, but a dynamic force within the EU, thanks largely to the current economic boom which offers so much hope to my generation. The young people of Ireland are aware not only of our humble beginnings but also of how much has changed, and as we approach the new millennium you can witness the new-found self-confidence and assurance of Ireland's young. We know we can hold our own among any of the world's graduates, we are as vibrant and dynamic as our nation, educated and ambitious in our quest for success.

Success is a strange thing. Years ago success was a nice, secure, pensionable job or a wedding ring. Fortunately the definitions have changed with the attitudes and marriage is no longer the be-all and end-all for women. However, the pensionable and secure job has also vanished, leaving young people well aware of the need for education and the immeasurable value of versatility. As a result the life-plans many of us now hold seem very ambitious to older generations: but ambition is a must in the highly competitive labour market, those without plans fall through the cracks, this is a fact of life we deal with every day.

We are aware that along with all the success Ireland has enjoyed in recent years, there are the pitfalls of constantly moving goal posts, stress and pressure with which some cannot cope. The first big hurdle we encounter is the Leaving Certificate. By the end of 6th year, I was so glad I hadn't really known the awful extent of it at the beginning. If I had, no-one and nothing could have persuaded me to do it. The scramble for points worsens every year and simultaneously the suicide and drop-out rates continue to climb. Personally not even the lure of success could have persuaded me to re-sit my exams and fortunately for me I had no need to. I never knew whether to admire or pity those brave enough to repeat.

Everyone agrees something has to be done, but nobody seems to be able to come up with a viable alternative. Are we just supposed to sit by and watch more and more young people, who have so much to offer society, collapse under the strain of what is just one exam? There have to be better ways of determining intelligence, ability and suitability for employment than this. Besides, what happened to education for its own sake and love of learning, why must education be so job-market oriented?

Most of those who are actually sitting the exams and are part of the educational system feel there must be a better way of evaluating our ability.

In many ways the youth of today are very different to their predecessors and it is our attitudes more than anything else which distinguish us from the rest of the population. The lifestyles of the rich and famous to which, thanks to the media, we bear constant witness, have definitely left an impression on the Irish psyche. For so long we were a poor country in comparison with much of Western Europe, now not only can we hold our own, but are determined to outstrip them. We are perhaps more materialistic than at any other time, we not only want the best but we want it now, we are true products of a consumer society. The plethora of designer labels and high street stores are a manifestation of the attitude. We measure success by material items such as cars and addresses, clothes and jobs. Social status is of maximum importance, value judgements are made using such things and not one of us wants to be seen as not good enough.

I have to say I don't think this is a particularly good thing about my generation, we should perhaps appreciate that other things also make you successful, but in the end everyone equates success with material gain and material gain with happiness.

As a woman I find that the idea of 'success' often leaves me with a sneaking suspicion that an executive job is not really what would make me happy. After having this discussion many times with some good friends, all of whom are in third-level education, we came to a rather discomfiting conclusion. After all this time and all the hard work put in by all branches of feminism, after all the bra-burning and court cases related to equal pay, eventually my friends and myself want the same thing as most women 50 years ago wanted. Despite all my education and my firm belief in my (and indeed all women's) self-sufficiency, ultimately I and all my friends (with one exception) dream of the white wedding, the picket fence and the children.

The only notable and huge difference between the majority of women in my grandmother's generation and myself is that I definitely intend to have a career first. I want to spread my wings and experience many things *before* I settle down, but in the final analysis I want a secure and fulfilling relationship. Even in acknowledging that fact, my friends and I all admitted to also feeling a not inconsiderable spurt of guilt. We are letting the side down are we not? Have we committed some treasonous act towards all the women who have gone before us, from the Pankhursts to Erica Jong to Andrea Dworkin, in admitting such a thing? We *know* we can be whatever we choose to be, we know we have all the opportunities at our feet and now that women have proved they are as capable and deserve the same treatment and chances as men, we are happy to accept our roles as nurturers with an almost clear conscience.

Whatever else, I do believe that women in my age group (early twenties) have learned something very important from the experiences of women in the 1980s. No-one can have it all. In the 1980s so many women, convinced they could, decided to attempt to juggle all the balls: marriage, a career, children, a social life. In the long run something had to give and it often seemed to be the woman's sanity. So we have accepted that sacrifices are most definitely in order, the best part about this is, that the choice of what to sacrifice is all ours.

The interesting thing is, while it does not have to be the career, it seems this is what most are willing to sacrifice. I was lucky enough to have a full-time mother and believing, as I do, that I would have lost out if she had not always been there when I was small, how could I provide anything less for any children I might have? More and more young women are realising that giving your child the best involves staying at home. It is sad that in many cases, economic reasons force young mothers to go out to work. I do not necessarily feel it has to be the mother who stays at home, it is obviously sensible that the parent in the higher-paying job should go out to work. However when asked many of us feel that a restructuring of the labour market is very necessary, not only for allowing full-time parenthood, but even to aid the unemployment problem. It is time to admit full-time, pensionable jobs are no longer really necessary. Job sharing, restrictions on overtime and personal pension plans are all going to be an integral part of working in the new millennium, if we are to ensure the bottom does not fall out of the economy.

In general, I think the young people of Ireland have adjusted to a very changed country without really being aware of the changes that have taken place. We do not share the sense of loss that grips my mother's generation because it is difficult to mourn that which you did not know. Rather than feeling Ireland has lost a great deal, I believe we have gained so much, culturally as much as in any other department. For me our membership of the EU and subsequent fears of loss of identity have served to reinforce those things that make us uniquely Irish, despite the sociological and economic phenomenon of homogenisation. Naturally the more integrated the global economy the more similar the trends in countries, but history cannot be forgotten because of some treaties and legislation, as a people we have experienced things that were distinctly Irish and that is a trend my generation believe will continue. We have such a rich and diverse culture; it's one of our selling points as far as the tourism industry is concerned. From a very cynical point of view that would be our main motivation in ensuring we do not lose our native flavours, but there are those with a much less world-weary attitude who believe we will not lose them because they are inherent within us, I am one of those people.

We, as a group, have great hopes and expectations, not only for ourselves, but also for our country. As we strive for bigger and better things, we bring the nation with us. Ireland was always ten years behind everyone else, and even now, despite the rapid changes being wrought, we have some catching up to do and despite the youth's optimism for the bright future, some of us are also aware of the pitfalls that exist. We as the future leaders of, and spokesmen for, Ireland, wish for more foresight from the current leaders. We seem to be heading straight down the path that both Britain and the US took before they had to vigorously campaign to go 'Back to Basics'. It would seem prudent to stop certain things before they progress that far. Among the young people there is a certain sense of our social responsibility, something which our predecessors of the 1980s seem to have lacked. Larger issues than the mere economic welfare of our people need to be discussed.

We, just like every other generation that has gone before us, are concerned with the future of the environment, the future of social integration, the future educational system and the future job situation. We do not want to see further deterioration of our air and water quality; we do not want to be like the Japanese with their filter masks and cramped living quarters, or like the majority of continental countries where the tap water is undrinkable. We want spaces for the children to play safely and various species of animals to be alive and well. It is imperative that the government does more to protect our habitat.

We also do not want to see a segregated society with bitter racial tensions. We may have finally ended one bloody and bitter conflict, why do we wish to start another? The fledgling but apparent ghettoisation of the inner city is worrying. We do not want a repeat of LA or Brixton. The racism that was latent in Ireland for so long is coming to the fore with vengeance, as my mother has discussed, and with it comes some very frightening scenarios. The gruesome murder of the black American in Texas earlier this year may seem unreal in its horror, but if we are not careful, we might end up in exactly the same place.

Ultimately I think my generation is very different to my parents' generation and even to those of our age a decade ago. We would like to think we are more aware and informed of the dangers and the good in society. Perhaps it is the arrogance of youth that makes us believe we can change things and make a difference, but somebody needs to believe they can if change is to happen. I would like to believe my generation is more tolerant of that which is different, we have learnt to live with gay couples and single mothers, soon we will learn to live with different ethnic groups. There are of course those who will be scathing of the idealism of youth, but in order to better things an ideal is needed. My generation, whatever we end up being dubbed, have certain ideals we would like for society: a cure for AIDS and all types of cancer, harmony, prosperity, they may not be so different to those things for which previous generations have wished, the question is will we achieve what we want and what changes will ensue in Ireland? My biggest hope is that as we go into the millennium we ensure the good outweighs the bad, and we retain our belief in our ability to make things happen.

Conclusion

I have lived in Ireland for 31 years – so much has happened, there have been so many changes. A neighbour of mine summed it up for me when she said, "Changes are all for the better, we are a better people, the young have no hang ups any more, they are educated, able, confident and vibrant, they are more caring than we ever were, they may not be regular church goers, but we all went to church on orders – what good did it do? We were full of fear – fear of God, fear of sin, guilt, we had no confidence in ourselves, we were brain-washed by the Church – everything we thought of, said or did, was crowned with the word sin. May the Catholic Church never again get the power it had until the 1980s. We are not living in the Ireland of de Valera and McQuaid. We have moved on, we are not the inward-looking, peasant Irish any more, we have at last become part of the wider world – we are right there and we are international."

Indeed Ireland has metamorphosised from a predominantly agricultural, rigidly Catholic, reasonably educated, diffident, poor and rural society to a highly technological, loosely ecumenical, highly educated, confident, wealthy and urban society in a very short period of time. Some of the changes however, were gradual while others appear to have taken place at an electrifying speed, especially during the 1990s. One can attribute these quick cultural changes, most of them much needed and highly desirable, to five basic factors.

- Ireland's membership of the EU.
- A higher level of participation in third-level education.
- The explosion of technology and our leap into the age of information.
- European and global travel and exposure to other cultures.
- The unprecedented wealth and prosperity of this decade.

The famous land of the welcomes so distinctly and proudly identified with St Patrick and the shamrock is now the land of the Celtic Tiger.

Politically-correct language coupled with media power and 'brainwashing', and the emphasis on making large amounts of money, have contributed to a gradual decline of some well-established, beneficial values and traditions of Irish society. There appears to be an inhibition in articulating our concerns about some undesirable aspects of our society. Surely the very education that is empowering a large majority of the people should also enable us to hold on to, cherish and nurture some worthwhile "old-fashioned" Irish attributes which collectively and effectively contributed to the growth and emergence of a very prosperous Ireland. There is such an emphasis on the rights and needs of the individual, mé féin, myself.

I can only hope that we will be able to distinguish the good from the bad, and draw upon the experiences of other societies while at the same time retaining the Irish individuality, charm, humour, pride, concern for the poor and under-privileged (locally, nationally and globally) and above all, the good quality of life in general. There is every reason to believe that the young generation of today – the children of the late-1970s and those born afterwards who grew up in a very different, almost modern Ireland – will march into the millennium without the excess baggage of 'Catholic guilt' of the Ireland into which I came and will have moved beyond the materialism of the 1990s.

This book is mainly the expression of my deepest concerns for the 'genuine' refugees and asylum-seekers who were attracted to this country just two or three years ago because of its prosperity. As an immigrant who has lived here for such a long time with great pride and without any difficulty, I appeal to the people, the Minister for Justice, his Department and the Government to be just, fair and considerate towards the people who are seeking refuge and asylum here. All human beings, rich and poor, black and white, able and disabled, educated and un-educated have dignity and feelings – please do not humiliate them. Mahatma Gandhi who was a victim of racism in South Africa said, "How can one human being take pleasure in humiliating another?" Racism is evil and must be nipped in the bud.

The life of the bouncing young Celtic Tiger of the 1990s may not be a long and healthy one and it would be a pity if the fundamental nature and character of the Irish nation and her people, which attracted me to stay here in the first place, were sacrificed to it. Enjoy the prosperity by all means but take time out to reflect on the core values of the society of yesteryear that have seen us through many difficult periods since independence. Values that enabled us to hold our heads high and become the envy of many other, wealthier nations. The caring and the compassion, the smiles and the welcome, the humour and the song – let these not end up in the jaws of the Celtic Tiger. This is my hope.

Appendix 2

Definitions

Refugee

Someone who owing to a well-founded fear of being persecuted for reason of Race, Religion, Nationality, Social Group, Political Opinion is outside the country of his nationality and is unable, or owing to such a fear, is unwilling to avail himself the protection of that country.

1951 Geneva Convention Definition

The Irish Legal Definition is the same in the Refugee Act 1996 but adds Trade Union Membership and Sexual Orientation.

Asylum-Seeker

Person at border or within country who seeks protection and applies for recognition as refugee to Department of Justice, Equality and Law Reform.

Temporary Leave to Remain

Status given to individuals who do not fully meet UN definition but strong humanitarian reasons exist.

There is no formal definition in Irish Law.

Programme Refugee = Quota

Individual or group accepted on basis of government decision as refugees prior to arrival, in response to UNHCR request, e.g. Bosnians and Vietnamese.

Convention Refugee = Statutory

Those asylum applicants accepted by the State after a determination process (initial or appeal stage) as fulfilling UN Convention definition.

Appendix 3

Legal Instruments

Article 14 of UN Declaration of Human Rights 1948

(1) Everyone has the right to seek and to enjoy in other countries asylum from persecution.

(2) This right may not be invoked in the case of prosecutions genuinely arising from non-political crimes or from acts contrary to the purposes and principles of the United Nations.

UN Convention on the Elimination of all forms of Racial Discrimination 1965

Under this Convention, states are pledged:

> to engage in no act or practice of racial discrimination against individuals, groups of persons, or institutions, and to ensure that public authorities and institutions do likewise;
>
> not to sponsor, defend or support racial discrimination by persons or organisations;
>
> to review Government, national and local policies and to amend or repeal laws and regulations which create or perpetuate racial discrimination;
>
> to prohibit and put a stop to racial discrimination by persons, groups and organisations;
>
> and
>
> to encourage integrationist or multi-racial organisations and other means of eliminating barriers between races, as well as to discourage anything which tends to strengthen racial division.

This convention was adopted on 21 December 1965 by the general assembly of the United Nations. It has been ratified by all the Member States of the EU, and by around 150 nations worldwide. Ireland has signed the Convention subject to ratification. The Government position is that ratification will quickly follow the enactment of the Equality and Equal status legislation.

Report of the National Co-ordinating Committee,
1997 European Year against Racism

Dáil Motion on Racism, Tuesday 16 December 1997

The Minister for Justice, Equality and Law Reform (Mr O'Donoghue) moved:

that Dáil Éireann –

1. affirms, in accordance with the principles of international human rights law, the right of everyone to live free of violence, discrimination or harassment on the basis of race, colour, national or ethnic origin or membership of the traveller community;
2. condemns sentiments and manifestations of racism, xenophobia and anti-Semitism as inimical to respect for the dignity of all human beings and particularly deplores hostile statements or acts directed against those from other countries seeking refuge in the State;
3. supports all appropriate efforts to promote harmonious relations between different groups characterised by reference to race and related factors;
4. notes:
   (i) that the Minister for Justice, Equality and Law Reform, building on the work of his predecessors, has initiated the Employment Equality Bill which would, *inter alia*, make provision for the promotion of equality and the prohibition of discrimination and harassment in employment and related areas on the basis of factors including race, colour, nationality, ethnic or national origin or membership of the traveller community; and

   (ii) the Government's stated commitment to bring forward an Equal Status Bill which would have a similar effect in relation to non-employment areas;

5. requests the Government, following enactment of the legislation referred to in paragraph 4, to take steps for the ratification of the International Convention for the Elimination of All Forms of Racial Discrimination, adopted by the General Assembly of the United Nations on the 21 December 1965;
6. notes the measures taken in Ireland resulting from the Resolution of the European Union Council of Ministers designating 1997 as European Year against Racism;
7. commends the efforts of voluntary groups who have taken initiatives to combat racism and xenophobia;
8. urges the earliest possible implementation of the Refugee Act 1996.

The all-party motion was agreed.

Parliamentary Debates, Dáil Éireann, Vol. 485 No. 2

Refugee Act 1996

The main provisions of the Act are to give effect to:

1. the United Nations Convention relating to the Status of Refugees (1951)
2. the Dublin Convention of 1990, which determines the state responsible for examining applications for asylum among Member States of the European Union.

In addition the Act makes provision for the appointment of a Refugee Applications Commissioner and a Refugee Appeal Board.

Appendix 4

Refugees and Asylum Seekers: some statistics

Data for this appendix has been reproduced, with kind permission, from Michaël Begley's book *Back to the Roots: a needs assessment study of asylum seekers in Ireland* (Spiritan Publications, Dublin, 1998)

Highest Level of Formal Education among Refugees and Asylum-Seekers – Ireland, 1992–1998

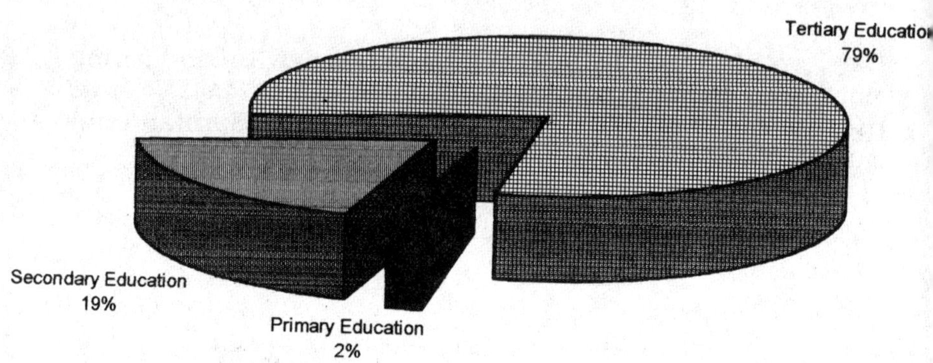

Religious Affiliations among Refugees and Asylum-Seekers – Ireland, 1992–1998

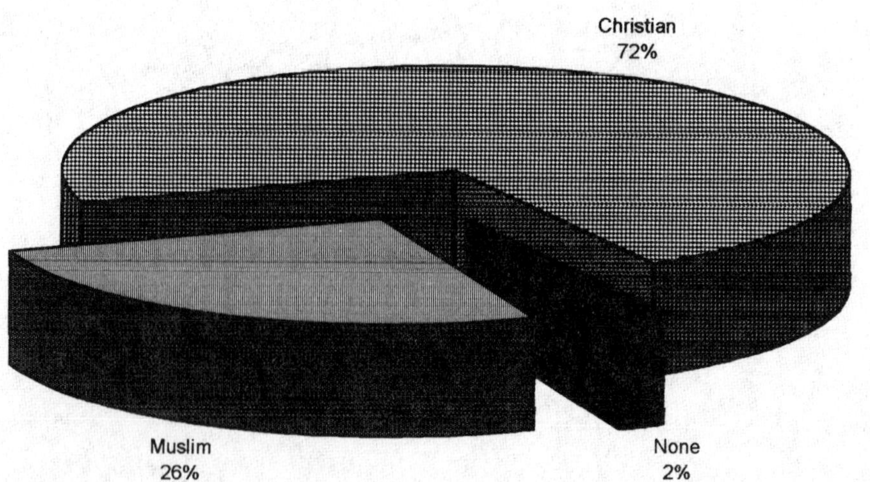

Asylum Applications – Ireland, 1992–1998

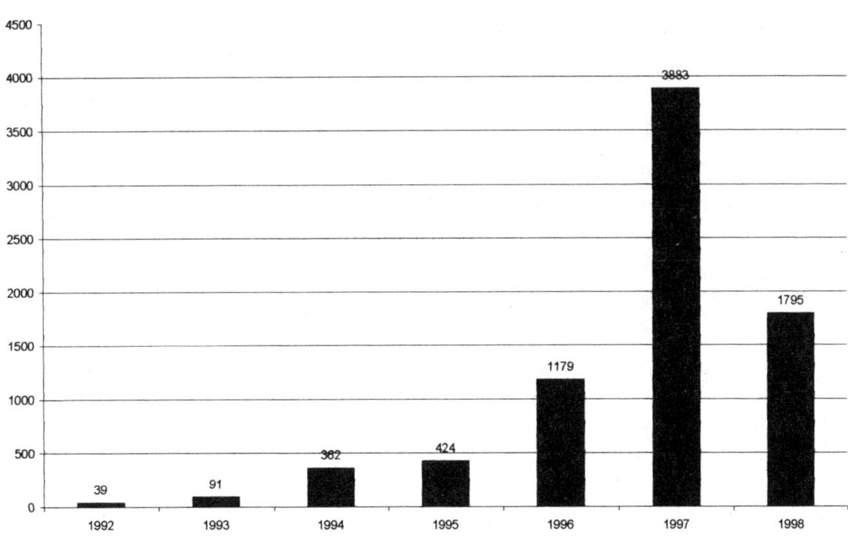

Asylum Determinations – Ireland, 1992–1998

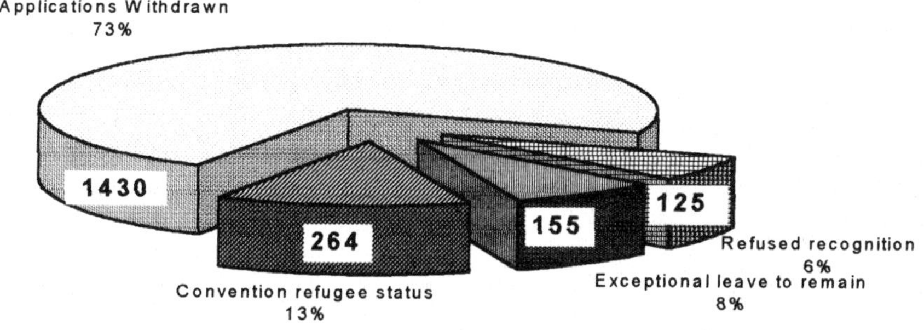